Hello There, We've Been Waiting for You!

LAURIE B. ARNOLD

PROSPECTA PRESS

For information about permission to reproduce selections from this book, contact:
Prospecta Press
P.O. Box 3131
Westport, CT 06880
www.prospectapress.com

Book and cover design by Barbara Aronica-Buck, www.bookdesigner.com

Paperback ISBN:978-1-935212-51-5
Ebook ISBN: 978-1-935212-61-4

*To the real-life Madison for your sunny inspiration;
and to Steve, my number one champion,
and the best husband and story editor I could ever dream of*

Chapter One

I didn't know anything about the magic yet. I only knew my life would never be the same. It was the summer before sixth grade and there I was, a prisoner in the front seat of my grandmother's sparkly gold Cadillac beast. She barreled at the speed of fear, north toward New Mexico on the dusty desert highway. We streaked past a blur of scrub brush and tumbleweeds. Compared to where I'd lived on Bainbridge Island in Washington State, it looked like I'd landed on the moon.

"Honey, this isn't what either of us wished for, but I'm sure we'll make the best of it."

I stared out the passenger window trying not to cry as I watched a tumbleweed skitter across the sand.

"And who knows? We might even have ourselves a little fun. How'd you like to be transformed into a vision of beauty? I happen to be quite the expert."

She shook her bouncy blond curls.

If she thought she was going to turn me into her clone, she had another think coming. I'm a soccer-player girl, not a dress-up girly-girl.

"Madison, darling, if you're ignoring me because I picked you up a teensy bit late, you'll have to get over it."

A *teensy* bit late? She'd arrived at the El Paso Airport an *hour and a half* after my plane got in, looking as if she was trying to be some movie star hot-shot hiding behind giant dark sunglasses. She'd sashayed in on super-spiky red high heels, wearing a matching mini-skirt. With barely a "hello" she whisked me off to my brand new life.

"Will Grandpa Jack be at your house?" I asked.

"Not until Saturday. He only comes around two weekends a month—which is just enough for me. So until then it'll be just us girls."

I wished more than anything I could turn back time.

My grandmother took control of the steering wheel with her knees as she drew on fresh red lipstick. Then she cranked up the music on her car's CD player. At the top of her lungs she sang along to "Dancing Queen" ten times straight.

The weirdest thing? So far she hadn't once mentioned my mom.

Here's the funny thing about life. Sometimes stuff happens that makes you want to erase a moment forever. But life isn't like pencil marks on paper. It can't be erased even if you make a gazillion wishes every night on the brightest star.

The thing I wanted to erase? Okay, I *hate* talking about it, but I guess I'll just come right out and say it. Four months and twenty-three days ago my mom died. Her heart just stopped beating and, almost in a snap, she was gone.

The night she died I moved in with my best friend, Violet, and her family and stayed with them until school let out. Then Violet flew off to spend the summer with her favorite grandmother in Paris, and I boarded a plane to El Paso, forced to face my new life sentence.

By late afternoon we pulled into Truth or Consequences. It was like a ghost town. There wasn't a soul on the streets, just row after row of thrift shops selling everyone's cast-offs. I thought about climbing into one of the display windows with a "for sale" sign slung around my neck and waiting for someone to buy me for a bargain.

"How'd you like to see where you'll be going to school in August?" she asked.

"Is it where my mom went when she was a kid?"

"No. They tore that dump down years ago. It was crumbling to pieces."

Kind of like my life.

My grandmother sped onto a desolate road, bordered by total colorless nothingness. In the middle of a flat field was a single hulking windowless brick building. Truth or Consequences Middle School. This was a place that would never crumble. It was built like a maximum-security prison.

"Okay, honey. Are you ready to hightail it home?" Then she hit the gas.

Home? I couldn't imagine I'd ever feel at home anywhere other than in my shingled house in the woods on Bainbridge Island. And I especially couldn't ever in a million years imagine feeling at home living with my grandmother.

I remembered the first time I met her. I was five. My mom and I were on a road trip, passing through New Mexico.

When she answered the door I'd said, "Hi, Grandma."

She just about choked on her chewing gum.

"Madison, darling, do I call you Granddaughter?" she'd asked.

"No," I'd said.

"What do I call you?"

"Madison."

"And why do I do that, do you suppose?" She'd held my chin in her hand and made me look her in the eye. It was weird.

"Because that's my name?"

"Yes, Madison is your name. And my name is Florida. Florida Brown. I don't want to hear you call me Grandmother, Grandma, Nana, Grandmumsy, Granny or anything else that might make me feel the slightest bit old. I work very hard not to look old. Do you understand?"

I'd nodded, even though I didn't understand at all. My mom rolled her eyes.

My grandmother—excuse me—*Florida*, turned onto Grape Street, gunned her Cadillac, and shot up the driveway to her red brick house. She hit the brakes and stopped inches short of the garage door. On it hung a black iron cutout of a cowboy ready to lasso any car that dared to come too close.

I breathed in a little courage and reached for the door handle.

"Stay here. Don't get out," she whispered.

Florida fiddled with the rearview mirror, swiveling it to get a better angle on someone lurking at the house next door.

Was it a prowler? A murderer on the loose?

Chapter Two

"Okay, now you can look. She's not watching."

I peeked over at the neighbor's house. An African American lady about Florida's age was checking her mail. She wore layers and layers of clothes, even a pair of sweatpants pulled over her jeans. Her kinky jet-black hair was twisted in a tangle of braids encircling her head, ending in a fat topknot. Her skin was the color of coffee, and she was singing so loud I could make out the words even through our closed car window with the air conditioner on high.

"That woman is possessed by the devil," Florida told me. "Number one rule? Stay away. She's crazy as a loon."

She did look a little odd, wearing all those thick layers in the hot New Mexico sun. I watched as she slid an enormous stack of mail into a small beat-up leather fanny pack. I couldn't imagine how it all fit. Weird.

We waited for her to go back inside before we got out of the car.

Inside Florida's house it was dark as a cave. My eyes struggled to adjust after the bright New Mexico sunlight.

I followed my grandmother to the end of the hall, my suitcase clickety-clacking behind me on the hard tile floor.

"Prepare to behold a true vision of sheer beauty." She said it in the most dramatic way, as if she was revealing some well-kept secret of the universe. Then she opened the door.

"Ta-da!"

My new bedroom was pink. The bedspread, the curtains, the throw rug, the fluffy stuffed poodle, and the ballerina lamp. It was all cotton-candy pink.

"Isn't it divine? I bought the entire ensemble on *The Shopping Mall Network*."

I hate pink.

It's true that plenty of girls like it, and that's perfectly okay with me. I would never hold it against them. Give me any other color in the universe and I'm happy.

"Honey, isn't this room just you all over?"

"It's, uh, nice. Thanks." What could I have said without hurting her feelings?

Then I noticed a wall of boxes stacked to the ceiling.

"Don't worry about those. They're just a few must-have goodies I bought from my shopping shows. Or I thought they were must-haves when I bought them." Florida shrugged. "But I might need them some-day. You never know! Now, are you ready for a TV dinner? Glazed turkey Lean Cuisine?"

"No thanks. I'm not hungry," I said.

"We could watch the *Shop 'Til You Drop Channel* together. They're featuring hair accessories." Her eyes sparkled and gleamed as if hair accessories were the best things in the entire universe.

"I think I'll just unpack and go to sleep." I slung my backpack onto the girly-girl bed.

"It's awfully early, but suit yourself. If you need me, I'll be looking for treasures on my shopping shows. Nighty-night."

I shut the door and sat on what was once my mom's bed. I pulled my most prized possessions from my backpack. My drawing book and colored pencils. My good-luck soccer ball that my whole team had signed after I scored the winning goal in the championships. My two favorite framed photos—one of Violet and me in our soccer jerseys, and the other one of my mom and me at the beach, our matching hair blowing in the wind. I set them on the nightstand, beside the ballerina lamp.

At the bottom of my backpack was my mom's Washington State Ferry jacket. It was the one she'd worn at work, directing cars on and off the ferryboat that went back and forth between our island and downtown Seattle.

I unpacked my suitcase—mostly T-shirts, shorts, and blue jeans. Most of my stuff I'd left at Violet's house for safekeeping. Maybe I was trying to convince myself that moving in with Florida would only be temporary.

Even though it had just turned dark outside, I curled into a ball on top of the covers and buried myself under my mom's jacket. It smelled just like her. When my eyes were closed it was almost as if she were beside me. I inhaled the sweetness of cinnamon and butterscotch, waiting for the moon to rise in that same room where my mom had slept when she was a kid. I'm pretty sure she'd be horrified to know it was now baby-pink.

I couldn't sleep. My head was filled with thoughts I couldn't switch off. The weirdo lady next door. My best friend, Violet, in perfect Paris. My strange grandmother. My mom dying. Outside a dog howled and a man yelled bad words to make it stop. But loudest of all was the steady blare of the TV as Florida flipped through the channels, searching for something to buy.

My second biggest wish was that the bottomless pit in my heart would go away. My first biggest? That I'd wake up and all of this was really just a super-strange dream.

But the next morning I was still in a cotton-candy-pink bedroom on Grape Street. Living in Truth or Consequences, New Mexico, with Florida Brown was my strange new reality.

My mom used to say, "Today is the first day of the rest of your life." I was pretty sure that this was the first day of what would be the worst life in all of recorded history.

Chapter Three

When I wandered into the living room the next morning it couldn't have been later than seven-thirty. Florida was already on the phone, buying something called a Belly Buster from the *Shop 'Til You Drop Channel*. Strap it around your middle and it was guaranteed to melt away your fat.

She cupped her hand over the telephone. "I've been on a little shopping spree this morning. Early bird catches the bargains! Now watch this, honey. You'll be impressed."

The man on the TV picked up his ringing phone. He looked like he was made out of plastic.

"We have Florida from Truth or Consequences, New Mexico, on the line," he said. "We've missed you, Florida, my friend!"

The TV host actually knew my grandmother and was having a conversation with her right on TV!

Florida giggled in her movie star voice. "Alan Stone, how are you?"

She was flirting with him. Gross.

"Alan dear," she went on. "I really don't have much of a belly to bust, but it will be fantastic to have this during the holidays when the gals bring over their sweet, high-calorie treats. Oh, and Alan—I have a teeny favor to ask. Could you give a little shout-out to my darling eleven-year-old niece, Madison?"

Niece?!

The TV host looked right into the camera. "Hello there, Madison. This is for you and your Aunt Florida." Then he blew us a kiss. Right on television. It was freaky. Thank goodness none of my friends back in Washington watched the shopping shows.

"We both send big lovey-dovey kisses back, Alan! Mwah!" Florida said. Then she hung up the phone.

I stared at her as if she was a space alien. "I'm not your niece."

"Of course you're not. But we don't want Alan Stone thinking I'm old enough to be a *grandmother*, for goodness sake. Don't worry. It was only an itsy-bitsy teeny-weenie little white lie."

I didn't care what color the lie was. A lie was still a lie. Unless you're trying to spare someone's feelings. That's what my mom always said. Saying you're too young to be a grandmother when you really were one didn't exactly qualify. That's what I thought, but I stopped myself from saying so.

I thought I'd spend the rest of the day in my room, so I stood up from the sofa. My grandmother pulled me back down by the hem of my T-shirt.

"Don't leave yet, honey. Next is a special on designer scarves."

In five minutes flat she bought seven of them—one in every color of the rainbow. Then she flicked back and forth between a whole bunch of shopping channels.

"So much to buy, so little time . . ."

As she picked up the phone to order a half-dozen jeweled watches, the doorbell rang. Florida got up to answer the door. "Who could that be?"

Uh-oh. Was it the crazy lady?

A redheaded guy with a scruffy beard stood on the other side of the doorway, holding a clipboard. Behind him was a pimply-faced teenager.

"May I help you boys?" Florida's voice was all dramatic, like she was the queen of her castle.

"Special delivery, Mrs. Brown," said the guy with the clipboard. "It's your brand-new flat-screen TV."

"I don't recall ordering a new TV," Florida said.

"Your name and address are on our delivery slip, Mrs. Brown." He held up his clipboard as evidence.

"Well, bring it in," Florida shrugged.

I peered outside to watch them struggle to unload a giant box from the back of a dented old delivery truck. Painted on the side were faded gold curlicue letters that said MIRACLE MOVERS.

As they rolled it up the walkway on a dolly, Florida bounced like a kid on Christmas morning. "Who knows? Maybe I did order it. Well, guess it's meant to be."

How could anyone forget ordering a new *television set*? She must have bought a lot of stuff to have something that massive slip her mind.

"The name's Mike," the redheaded guy said to me once he and his partner ripped open the box in the living room. "How about giving us a hand, Squirt?"

He seemed pretty nice, so I didn't mind him calling me that.

"Why don't you pull all the cords out of the plastic bags while we haul the old TV out to our truck, Squirt?"

"Mind holding the pliers for a minute, Squirt?" he asked when they fiddled with the wires to hook up the giant new flat-screen.

"Hey Squirt, how about handing me one of those remotes so I can show you both how to use this thing?"

There were two remote controls. They were thin and black with five big colored buttons, plus a whole bunch of little silver buttons. Possibly the most confusing things I'd ever seen.

"I highly recommend stashing one of these babies in a safe place. Just in case."

Just in case what?

"Here's the deal," Mike explained. "This is no ordinary TV. It's a

MegaPix 6000 picture-in-picture flat-screen that lets you keep an eye on six shows at a time."

"Perfect! Now I can watch all six of my favorite shopping shows at once. This is the happiest day of my life," said Florida. "How much did I pay for this treasure?"

"As far as I know, not a cent."

"It was *free*? Well, maybe I didn't order it after all. Maybe one of my shopping shows sent it since I'm such a devoted customer. Like a bonus prize."

Really? Somehow I doubted it.

Mike explained how the MegaPix 6000 worked. He showed Florida how to push the colored buttons so she could choose the six programs she wanted to watch. Then he demonstrated how to move a TV program that was playing in one of the five little frames at the top, down to the main part of the screen.

"There are a few other important features I need to go over with you," he said.

"Mike, darling, I know it's probably hard to believe since I'm sure I don't look a day over 29, but I started using remote controls long before you were born. I can take it from here. Is there something I should sign?"

He shrugged and handed her the clipboard. "You might want to read the fine print on the contract first."

Florida laughed. "Oh my, whoever reads these things?" Without looking at one word of it, she signed her name.

He tore off a copy and set it on the table beside the remotes.

"You do know that the MegaPix puts you in the action like no TV you've ever had before?" Mike said.

"Of course I do! It's high-definition. They're all like that," Florida said.

"Not exactly. This is a one-of-a-kind TV."

Whoever heard of a one-of-a-kind TV?

"There is something you really ought to know, Mrs. Brown—"
But Florida cut him off. "Mike? Trust me. I can take it from here."
"Okay then," he shrugged. "It's all yours."

He and his pimply-faced partner packed up the cardboard. As they hauled it to the door, Mike stopped to whisper in my ear.

"Good luck, Squirt."

Then he winked.

A cold shiver shot up my back.

Chapter Four

I could tell this was kind of a holy moment for Florida. She pulled out a can of Orchid Oasis room freshener.

"Let's welcome the new TV with the divine scent of happiness."

And then she sprayed.

I remember smelling a real orchid once. It was the prettiest flower I'd ever seen. I'd leaned in to take a whiff and expected the scent of something wonderful, but it smelled exactly like—nothing. My mom said it was a good reminder that pretty on the outside doesn't always mean pretty on the inside.

Florida's Orchid Oasis spray didn't smell a bit like orchids. More like a public restroom that got cleaned up with sweet perfumey stuff after someone threw up in the toilet.

"Let's take this TV for a test drive." She patted the spot beside her on the sofa.

I sat down and watched her fingers work lightning-fast on the remote. In record speed she figured out how to get six shopping channels on the TV at once.

"My mission is to buy six fabulous things from six shopping shows in ten minutes. Here's the stopwatch. Ready? Go!"

I pushed the silver button on the stopwatch, and Florida flew into action. She punched in phone numbers for the shopping shows even faster than she'd worked the remote control. She knew them all by heart.

The first thing she bought was from the *Home Shopping Channel*. It was a blender powerful enough to grind a G.I. Joe into dust. Why anyone would ever need to do that, I haven't a clue.

The next three items she purchased? Two cases of Sunflower Blond hair dye; a Hamdogger, which made hamburgers in the shape of hotdogs; and a ceramic poodle for her collection. Where would she even put that poodle? Her shelves were already bursting with them.

"Time check," Florida said.

"Three and a half minutes to go." Three and a half minutes until I could go back in my room for the rest of the day.

"Ooh! Melt Away Your Wrinkles face cream!"

She called the *Beauty Channel* and ordered about a zillion cases of the stuff.

"Now we'll have enough for both of us," she said.

"I don't have wrinkles. I'm eleven."

"It's never too early to start taking care of your complexion, dear."

I was pretty sure I was trapped in a nightmare.

And the final thing she bought? A giant bag of hair bows.

"We've got to do something about that hair of yours, honey," she said as she made the phone call.

What is it about my hair? The last time my grandmother commented about it was at Violet's house, right before my mom's funeral. "Madison, darling," she'd said. "You've grown so much. I wouldn't have recognized you, except for that stick-straight mouse-brown hair!"

I hadn't known what to say. Given the situation, I was already sad enough without having to hear that. Besides, I *like* my hair. It is exactly the same as my mom's.

"Cool it, Florida," Grandpa Jack had said.

After that Violet and I stayed in her room playing Crazy Eights until we had to leave for the cemetery. Right after my mom died, talking with anyone but Violet made me cry.

"That's it," Florida said when she hung up the phone. "Time?"

I pushed the button on the stopwatch. "Nine minutes and forty-three seconds."

"Oh, I am *good!* This TV is the best thing that ever happened to me."

Wow. Really?

"Can I go to my room now?" I asked.

But Florida was fixated on the new TV and didn't answer. I'm not sure she even noticed when I left.

I sat on my pink bed and sketched a picture of Florida being hypnotized by her shopping shows.

And I wondered why redheaded Mike had wished me good luck. Did it have something to do with that new TV?

Chapter Five

"Well dear, I'm off to my job at the flower shop. There's a box of Froot Loops and peanut butter and jelly in the cupboard if you're hungry. Don't get into too much mischief. I'll be home by five." Florida slung a sparkly rhinestone purse over her shoulder.

I'd just wandered out of my room where I'd spent most of the day before drawing and wishing I had a different life. I was still in my PJs.

Right before she left, Florida kissed the new TV goodbye. Well, actually she got real close and blew it a kiss since she didn't want to smudge the screen with lipstick.

Wow. Here's how many times my grandmother has kissed me: zero. And there she was, kissing a TV. Not that I wanted her to kiss me—not at all—but I still thought it was weird. Almost as weird as her obsession with buying so many things from the shopping shows. Why does someone need that much stuff, anyway?

But I didn't mind spending the day alone. I wasn't in the mood to meet anyone new. Ever since my mom died, everyone I meet always asks me what happened. It's usually the first question after they've said, "I'm sorry." I'm thinking of having a little card printed up to hand out.

Hi! My name is Madison McGee. I'm eleven years old. My mom died in February from a heart attack. She was only 33.

The doctors were as surprised as anyone because they didn't know she had a problem with her heart.

P.S. Thank you for being sorry.
P.P.S. I never knew my dad, so please don't bother asking if he's alive. I have no idea.

Don't get me wrong. I appreciate people's concern, and I know they're curious. It just makes me too sad to talk about it.

So spending the day solo sounded perfect.

As soon as Florida left I helped myself to a bowl of cereal, sat on the sofa, and flipped through the channels on the MegaPix. It seemed like an ordinary TV to me, other than that picture-in-a-picture business.

I eventually found a rerun of my favorite TV show, *Just Jessica*. It was a show Violet and I both loved, and we really loved Carlee Knight, the girl who played Jessica LePew. I'd already seen the episode. It was the one where the eighth graders at Sunnyside Middle School put on a play of Cinderella. Just to be mean, the meanest girl of them all, Ashley, cast Jessica as the evil stepmother's housecat. They all treated Jessica like dirt because she was a famous movie star and they were jealous. Only her best friend, Curtis, stuck up for her. That's how it was in every show, and she always did her best to put up with a bad situation. Violet and I figured that in real life Carlee Knight was probably one of the nicest girls in the world.

After Jessica saved the day, which she did at the end of every episode, I turned off the TV. The back-up remote control and the contract for the MegaPix were still on the coffee table. I remembered what Mike had said about putting them in a safe place, so I stashed them in the bottom of my underwear drawer. Then I grabbed my soccer ball and went into the backyard.

Not much grew out there—only a few fat clumps of prickly cactus. I was extra-careful not to get too close to the neighbor lady's yard.

At first I used my soccer ball as a pillow and lay in the dirt. The backyard may have been drab and dreary, but the sky was beautiful. It was as blue as the feathers on a blue jay's back. Huge, puffy white picture-clouds floated through the air. One minute a cloud was the spitting image of an elephant, and then it morphed into a three-layer cake with whipped cream frosting. I even spied an angel with lacy white wings. Maybe it was a sign from my mom that she was watching over me.

When I finally got up to dribble my soccer ball around the yard, I caught the lady next door staring right at me from her back window. My heart tightened, and I pretended not to notice. Turning on my heels, I kicked the ball to the opposite end of the yard. The next time I peeked, she was gone. Creepy.

But if the lady next door was a weirdo, it's possible that the neighbor who lived behind Florida was even weirder. The whole yard was littered with rusty car parts and cast-off computers.

"Move, you stupid dog!"

A skinny man with greasy hair dragged the ugliest, mangiest dog I'd ever seen to the edge of his property, closest to my grandmother's yard.

The dog whined and howled. It was the same howl I'd heard the night before.

"Shut up, you idiot mutt!" The man spat in the dirt.

He chained the dog to an enormous old cracked computer monitor and then sped off in his rickety van, kicking up dust.

At first the dog snorted and growled. Then he got busy scratching his fleas. A few flies buzzed around his head. He lunged and snapped, but they zipped away.

Poor dog.

I dribbled my soccer ball closer so I could get a better look. The man sure was right about one thing. This dog was definitely a mutt. Maybe a little bit pit bull, a little bit bulldog, with a sprinkling of something that gave him wiry wisps of sticking-up fur. He was short and round with big, buggy eyes. Patches of his dirty white coat were missing. His crooked bottom teeth stuck out. The poor guy was badly in need of braces. Soon he got bored with fly-catching and went to work gnawing his front paw, drenching it with pools of gooey slobber.

I decided to prove to the dog that all humans weren't so mean. I squatted down in front of him. "Hi there, little buddy!" I made my voice sound as cheerful as possible.

The dog gave a friendly bark. Then he crawled toward me, dragging the heavy computer monitor behind him inch by inch.

I set my soccer ball down and let him sniff my hand.

"Here, boy. It's okay, I'll be your friend. I won't hurt you."

He thumped his tail. He almost seemed to be grinning. As I reached over to pat his head, he lunged at my soccer ball and popped it.

He popped my lucky soccer ball! I grabbed for it, thinking maybe I could patch it up, but the dog growled and snatched it back. Rip! Then that mangy mutt leaped to his feet and flung my flattened ball around like a dead squirrel.

"You're a bad, bad dog!"

The dog wasn't paying the slightest bit of attention to me. He was too busy digging a hole and burying his new trophy.

I fought back tears and ran into the house, slamming the door behind me. I wanted to get as far away from that nasty soccer-ball murderer as possible.

Chapter Six

The minutes ticked by like hours. I sat on the sofa with my sketchbook and drew the dog's prison mug shot. Prison is just where he belonged.

Then to cheer myself up, I sketched a picture of Violet and me feeding the Canada geese at Waterfront Park, back on Bainbridge Island.

When I grow up I want to be a famous artist. When I draw, my whole world becomes a magical kingdom of dots, lines, curves, and pictures. Then the rest of the world goes away.

Just as I was starting in on a drawing of the beautiful cloud angel, a horrible howl echoed in the backyard.

I peered out the sliding glass door. The mangy soccer ball assassin was tangled up in his chain, struggling to yank himself free. But the more he pulled, the harder the chain choked his neck.

I crept outside to get a closer look. The second he saw me, his howl changed to a pitiful whimper.

Would the crazy lady next door come out and save him? I glanced over there, but her curtains were now pulled shut. It looked like no one was home. Where did she go?

Even though that nasty dog had massacred my soccer ball, I couldn't let him die.

The chain cinched tighter around his neck and he gasped for breath.

It was time to face my fears. Being afraid of the dog wasn't that big a deal considering he was being choked to death by a chain.

"I'll help you, boy."

I kneeled beside him. The chain pulled tighter, and his whimpers turned to heavy panting.

"Calm down, boy. Everything's going to be okay."

I moved my hands toward his collar, praying he wouldn't bite. He looked up at me with sad, buggy eyes and panted harder. I slid my fingers under the chain, and he yelped with pain. It was way too tight. The only thing to do was to unhook it from the TV monitor and set him free.

The second I unclipped him he bolted like a shot across the yard, past the neighbor lady's house, and then he was out of sight.

Great. I'd saved the dog, and then I'd lost him.

"Here, boy! Here, boy!" I called for the longest time, but I couldn't even make out the jangling of the chain dragging behind him.

I gave up and went back into the house.

Should I call 911? Just as I picked up the phone, there was a crash at the back door.

The dog was leaping at the glass!

I threw open the sliding door and he practically knocked me flat onto the living room floor. He licked me all over as if I were a steak-flavored Popsicle. Okay, maybe the soccer ball murderer wasn't entirely bad.

It was then that I noticed the tag jingling on his collar. On it was stamped the name *Leroy*.

"You're a bad boy, Leroy," I told him as I scrambled to my feet. "You popped my soccer ball and ran away."

The dog hung his head and whimpered.

"Okay, I forgive you. This time."

He panted with happiness and licked my leg with wet doggy kisses of thanks.

"Want me to take off your chain?"

Leroy thumped his tail.

I led him back outside to the patio, slid the door closed behind us, and unclipped the rusty chain from his collar. Immediately he charged to the middle of the yard and began to turn in circles so fast he looked like a spinning top.

"Come here, Leroy! Here, boy!"

Leroy trotted right to me. Wow. He may have been goofy-looking but he sure was smart.

"Sit, Leroy. Sit, boy." He stared at me blankly. Okay, maybe he still had things to learn. I pushed down his butt and he sat.

Violet and I had once trained her dog Oscar to sit and stay. We'd used little dog biscuits to reward him every time he did something right. The problem was, I didn't have any dog biscuits. But I knew what might work. Froot Loops. But how could I leave Leroy to go get the box?

I clipped on his chain and hooked it to the chaise lounge on the patio. I grabbed the Froot Loops from the kitchen cupboard and by the time I returned, Leroy had made himself at home. He was sprawled on his back on the chaise lounge, as if he were vacationing in a Hawaiian resort. All he needed was a pair of sunglasses and a bottle of *Dog de Soleil* sunscreen.

It turned out Leroy was a big fan of Froot Loops. It didn't take him more than ten minutes to learn how to sit.

We moved on to "stay" pretty quickly. That one wasn't so easy. All he wanted to do was follow me wherever I went. I'd walk two steps and Leroy would walk two steps right behind me. I'd walk real fast across the yard and he'd follow like a shadow at my heels, scooting along the dirt on his butt.

"Leroy!" I'd say, making my voice sound stern.

He'd stare guiltily down at the ground. Then each time he'd look up and give me a big grin. Seriously. That dog could smile.

Because it was getting super-hot outside, I finally gave up trying to teach him to "stay." Since Florida wasn't home, I thought it wouldn't be so bad if he came into the house with me for just a little bit. Besides, he was the only friend I had—and at least he couldn't ask me any questions about why I had to move in with my grandmother.

The second I slid open the door, Leroy barreled inside. He raced through the house, skidding on the throw rug in the hall, then zipped back to the living room. I pleaded for him to stop, but he kept on going.

He sailed onto the sofa, knocking every cushion to the floor. Then he scampered into the kitchen, where he immediately scattered the trash. In ten seconds flat he licked up all the leftover scraps from Florida's TV dinner tray.

The more I yelled "stop" the faster he zoomed from room to room, knocking over lamps, chairs, and boxes of TV shopping stuff stacked in the hallway.

Then in one giant leap he practically flew onto the dining room table as if he were auditioning for the role of Super Dog. He skidded right into Florida's fake flower centerpiece. Just as he was about to snatch it in his jaws, it came to me. I yelled one of the only commands he knew.

"Sit! Leroy, sit!"

Leroy sat. Right in the middle of the dining room table. He eyed the box of Froot Loops, waiting for his reward. Then he smiled. Seriously smiled.

I sighed and gave him a few bits of cereal. How could I resist that grin?

The house was a disaster. I had to clean up before Florida came home. Leroy followed me as I tidied, mostly because I dropped a trail of cereal wherever I went. He happily sucked the pieces up like a vacuum cleaner.

As I was putting the last cushions back on the sofa, the TV switched on.

The remote control was clenched in Leroy's teeth.

"Come here, boy. Drop it. Drop it!"

Leroy wagged his tail. Drool oozed from his mouth and slid down the plastic. On the TV someone was selling underwear so tight it made ladies' butts look two sizes smaller.

I approached him super-slowly. He flung the remote back and forth just as he'd done with my soccer ball. I offered Leroy a Froot Loop. He dropped the remote control like a hot rock and inhaled the cereal.

The remote was totally drenched with doggie drool.

I sopped up the slobber with a paper towel. It was tricky cleaning around the buttons. As I dried them off, they'd get pushed in and the TV channels changed like mad.

One second someone was selling tight butt underwear, the next second it was some cheesy soap opera, and then a game show. The channels switched as fast as I wiped the buttons. As I cleaned around a small purple one, the sound on the MegaPix went dead.

A loud ping sounded, kind of like the noise an elevator makes before the doors slide open. A purple question mark appeared in the middle of the screen. Underneath it were some words.

Are you SURE you want to choose this channel?

If "yes" push ENTER again.

I'd never seen anything like that on a TV before.

"What do you think, boy? Should I push it?"

Leroy wasn't paying the slightest bit of attention. He was busy sniffing Florida's ceramic poodle collection.

Was this one of the features Mike the delivery guy had tried to warn us about?

The ENTER button was still wet with drool so I dried it off. I heard another ping. Suddenly my body turned as cold as stone. Everything went blurry, and a strange tingle shot through me. Seconds later, I realized I wasn't in Florida's living room anymore.

Chapter Seven

"Name?" A woman wearing a headset and holding a clipboard stared at me through sparkly winged glasses.

"You mean me?"

What had just happened? Giant video cameras and a zillion bright lights hung from the ceiling. Dozens of people scurried everywhere like an army of ants. People chattered and barked orders, but I don't think any of it sounded louder than the pounding of my own heart. Where in the world was I?

"Yes, you. What's your name?"

I was tongue-tied. Then I spotted the sign hanging over a fake living room. In bright green neon it said: SHOP 'TIL YOU DROP. *I'd zapped myself right into the TV studio of Florida's favorite shopping show!*

Mike wasn't kidding when he said the MegaPix 6000 put you in the action like no other TV.

"Come on, speak up! We're ready to go on the air."

"Uh, I'm Madison McGee."

The lady smacked her palm to her forehead. "Of course you are! Madison, we've been waiting for you!"

Then she spoke into her headset. "Margo! Makeup on Madison McGee!"

What was happening?

A woman with spiky purple hair zipped over and patted powder on my face. I was covered in a cloud of makeup dust that made my nose tickle.

"Don't squirm, kid. Those cheeks still need a touch of blush."

She brushed on some pink.

Was I going to be on television?

The clipboard lady looked me over. "Can we do something about the hair?"

Geez! What was the big deal about my hair?

"Not in the next two minutes."

Two minutes? I had to get out of there. Before I could think up a plan, some guy shoved a blue flowery dress over my head, right on top of my T-shirt and shorts. At least I still had the remote control. Could I push the same buttons to zap back to Florida's living room?

The clipboard lady broke into a broad grin. "Finally the folks in the front office got a clue. I've been badgering them for months to give us a kid to be our assistant product demonstrator. The audience is going to eat this up!"

Assistant product demonstrator? On a shopping show?

I wanted to tell her there'd been a terrible mistake, but my mouth had frozen shut. She kneeled down, talking a mile a minute.

"Okay, Madison, here's the deal. You'll meet the product representative for the Dirt Demon Deluxe over at the dirty carpet set. Her name is Libby. Our prop guy, Joe, will be off-camera. He'll signal for you to pick up one of the buckets filled with stuff that you'll throw on the carpet. Libby will vacuum it up. While she does, all you have to do is stand on the sidelines looking cute until Joe cues you to throw the next bucket. Got it?"

I could only nod my head. A zillion thoughts bounced through my brain like pinballs. Were they really going to put me on a shopping show? What if Florida came home and saw me on TV? How would I figure out which button to push on the remote control to get back to

Truth or Consequences? Could I even go back? And how in the heck was this even possible? The whole thing was super-freaky.

I positioned my thumb on top of the ENTER button. But I wasn't fast enough.

"I'll take that," said the clipboard lady as she snatched it from my hand. "Can't have you holding a remote control when you're on national television. How in the world did you get this from our Product Room, anyway?"

She handed it to a guy with a bright green lizard tattoo on his arm. Now what was I going to do?

It turned out I didn't have a second to think about it. Somebody pushed me over to the set with the carpet. Libby was already there, dressed up like she was going out for dinner. Who vacuums their floor wearing high heels and a tight black skirt?

"Are you nervous?" she asked me.

I nodded. And I was even more nervous about figuring out how to get out of there.

"I'm nervous too," Libby told me. "I've never been on television before."

And I'd never been *in* a television before.

Suddenly the clipboard lady looked frantic. "Where is he? Can somebody please get him here *now*! We're on in twenty seconds!"

"He's on his way," someone yelled back. I was curious who "he" was. Then in a burst of speed, a guy pushed a wheelchair into the studio. Sitting in it was the TV host that Florida loved and adored. Alan Stone!

He leaped from the wheelchair and plunked himself down on the sofa in the living room set. Margo dusted his face with powder and fluffed his hair.

"We're on in five-four-three-two-one," said the clipboard lady.

And then I was on live TV.

Chapter Eight

My heart fluttered fast as we waited for Alan Stone to introduce the Dirt Demon Deluxe. At least I didn't have to say anything. That part would be up to Libby.

"Good afternoon, my friends," Alan Stone said to the camera. "I have a little story I'd like to share about our next product.

"Just last week, my five-year old son Ben tried inviting a family of pigeons into our living room. How did he do this? He scattered ten pounds of birdseed all over our brand-new carpet and opened the sliding glass door. As luck would have it, I walked in before our house was invaded by birds. I pulled out our fancy vacuum cleaner, but it couldn't get all the birdseed up. Then I remembered that the Dirt Demon folks had given me one of these amazing vacuum cleaners to test. I pulled it out of the trunk of my car, plugged in in, switched it on, and guess what? It sucked up every last speck.

"But my friends, I always say 'Seeing is believing.' Libby has joined us today from the Dirt Demon Company and she's going to show us what a miraculous marvel of a machine this really is. Today we also have a special helper with us, young Madison McGee. After all, who knows how to dirty up a carpet better than a kid?"

Okay, that was rude. But I certainly wasn't about to say so right on TV because the cameras switched on to me that very second. My stomach was invaded by butterflies, and beads of sweat popped out on my forehead.

"What are we starting with, Libby?"

"Birdseed," she peeped so quietly I could barely hear.

Joe the prop guy pointed to a bucket of birdseed. That was my cue to pick it up.

"Exactly one bucketful of birdseed," Alan Stone said. "Now go for it, Madison. And give it all you've got!"

I took a deep breath. Here goes nothing, I thought. My hand shook as I scattered the birdseed on the carpet in front of the vacuum cleaner.

"How about that? She looks like she's been dirtying up carpets all her life!" Alan Stone thought he was really funny, but I didn't.

Libby vacuumed it up, then opened the vacuum cleaner and dumped everything it had sucked up right back in the bucket.

"Absolutely incredible," said Alan Stone.

I thought he was making too big a deal out of it. I mean, isn't that what vacuum cleaners are supposed to do?

"And what do we have next, Libby?" he asked.

"Sand," she barely whispered.

"What's that?"

"Sand," she squeaked louder. Her cheeks were turning sunburn-red.

Joe cued me, so I threw the sand. Some of it flew straight back into my eyes, and it was hard to keep them from looking all blinky while I was on camera. I waited until they cut back to Alan Stone and then rubbed them until they got teary enough to wash away the grit.

As Libby emptied the sand from the vacuum cleaner into the bucket, Alan Stone strolled over.

"Let's see this baby in action," he said.

Libby opened her mouth, but nothing came out.

While he went on and on about how great the vacuum cleaner was, she just stared at him. It was as if some strange love spell had overwhelmed her. Her mouth gaped like a goldfish. Her eyes turned glassy, and her skin changed to milky white. Then she pitched over backwards onto the floor in a dead faint. Right on television.

The cameras quickly moved in to show Alan Stone up close. He didn't say one single word about Libby dropping over. He just kept talking about the wonders of the vacuum cleaner. Joe the prop guy dragged poor Libby away.

The clipboard lady rushed over to me and whispered, "Madison, just keep going."

"What about Libby? Will she be okay?" I whispered back.

"We don't have time to worry about that. This is live TV. Listen carefully. You're going to dump the next bucket and then you'll do the vacuuming."

"Can't Alan Stone do that part?"

"Mr. Stone doesn't vacuum. It's up to you. And if you could say a few cute things along the way, even better." Then she scooted away.

I had to *talk*? On live TV? I heard the thump, thump, thump of my heart and was sure everyone else could too.

Joe gave me the signal. I picked up the next bucket, which was filled to the brim with little Legos. If I hadn't been so worried about having to talk on TV, showering the carpet with thousands of Legos would have been a blast. I tried to inhale a little courage and then froze.

The clipboard lady's face knotted up with worry. "Come on, you can do this," she whispered.

Could I? Then I realized maybe I could. I'd watched enough silly stuff on TV to know what to do. And to help take the edge off my nerves, I pretended I was only talking to Violet.

"Next up? A bucket of Legos," I said, straight to the camera before I scattered them like fat pieces of colorful confetti.

Phew. So far so good.

Then I switched on the vacuum, and it rattled and clacked, sucking them all up.

"Who wouldn't want to clean up Legos like this?" I said. "Kids would even want to do it themselves if they had a vacuum like this one." The clipboard lady smiled and gave me the thumbs-up. And I realized all the butterflies in my stomach had flown away.

I emptied all the pieces back into the bucket. It was filled to the top with Legos.

"That's what I call amazing," said Alan Stone.

"And that's what I call *cool*," I said.

"Take it from Madison McGee, my friends. The Dirt Demon Deluxe is *cool*. Very cool. Now who out there is ready to have something this cool in your very own home?"

"All it needs is an attachment to separate the Legos by size and color," I joked.

"Yes!" mouthed the clipboard lady as she and the prop guy gave each other a victory fist-bump.

Then the telephones began to ring off the hook.

On the other side of the studio rows of people sat at desks answering the calls. I wondered how many of them had talked to Florida one time or another. She probably knew them all by name.

Alan Stone scooted back to his living room set to chat with some of the callers. Here's what a few of them said:

"I love the Dirt Demon Deluxe, Alan. And I really love that little girl. She's so funny! I'll buy one. Oh, I mean the vacuum cleaner, not the little girl. But I'd buy her too if I could!"

"Alan, I live in a three-story house, so I'll take three. And wherever did you find that adorable kid?"

"I wasn't planning to buy a Dirt Demon, but now I've got to have one. Madison McGee is right. It *is* cool. And if she ever wants to come to my house to throw Legos on my carpet, I'd be happy to vacuum them up."

The clipboard lady grinned. "Kid, you're golden. Next stop, the Crispy Crunch dog food segment in Studio B. If I get my way, you'll never leave this place."

Chapter Nine

Before I could say a word, the guy who'd whisked in Alan Stone shoved me into the wheelchair and sped me out of the studio. On the way I noticed Libby was conscious again, sipping a glass of water.

"This is the fastest way to get around this place," he said as he charged down the hallway.

I clung to the chair, barely listening. I was keeping an eye out for the tattooed guy who had my remote control. We passed closed door after closed door.

At the end of the hall I saw the door to Studio B. Almost there. Just before the entrance, a door swung open. A sign said Product Room. Out came the guy with the lizard tattoo. We wheeled right past him.

"Stop!" I shouted. "I need to get something!" I crossed my fingers, hoping that's where my remote was.

"No time. Gotta keep on schedule!" We raced into Studio B.

I had to figure out a way to get back to that Product Room!

A curly haired guy with a headset and a clipboard pulled me out of the wheelchair.

"The name's Chris," he said as he shook my hand.

I figured he must have had the same job in this studio as the clipboard lady had in the other one.

"Here's the deal," he said. "Our show host, Sarah, is going to be chatting it up with Amy—the product rep—about Crispy Crunch dog food. When I cue you, you'll enter with a couple of puppies. Your job is to feed them the dog food and don't let them escape. Can you handle that?"

"No problem." I mean, how hard could that be? Just that morning I'd trained Leroy to sit using Froot Loops. And while I was feeding the puppies I'd figure out a way to get back to that Product Room.

Chris called "Five, four, three, two, one," and the cameras rolled. Sarah and Amy talked about the dog food and how nutritious and delicious it was.

At first they put me in a backstage room. Chris brought in two super-cute Golden Retriever puppies and they sniffed me all over. They must have smelled Leroy. When it was time to go on, they trotted right after me onto the set.

I sat on the floor next to an open bag of Crispy Crunch dog food, but all the puppies wanted to do was sniff me and chew on the blue flowered dress. They had zero interest in eating that dog food.

Sarah the host said something about how she'd seen them scarf down a huge bowl of the dog food backstage so maybe they were full, but I'm not sure she was telling the truth.

Okay, then the most bizarre thing happened. Sarah said to prove that the dog food was tasty she would eat it herself. She ripped open a bag, pulled out a handful, and stuffed it into her mouth.

"M-m-m. Crispy Crunch dog food is delicious!" She chewed and talked with her mouth full of the stuff. It was grosser than gross. "Tastes like gourmet burgers sprinkled with corn chips! Try some!"

She shoved the bag toward Amy. I could tell the last thing she wanted to do was to eat that dog food, even though it was her product they were selling.

"Go on!" Sarah insisted. "It's yummy!"

Amy took a bite. She gagged and looked like she was going to barf. Then she washed it down with a big gulp of water.

Meanwhile, the puppies managed to wiggle their noses up under my dress, smelling the pockets of my shorts. I suddenly realized what they were after. The Froot Loops! Thank goodness the cameras were on the two ladies devouring the dog food and not on me. I reached into my pocket and pulled out a handful of cereal I'd stashed in there when I was training Leroy. The puppies went bonkers, munching it up.

The camera zoomed in on me. I hoped it didn't get close enough to see that the puppies were actually eating cereal.

"Will you look at that? Those puppies are scarfing down the Crispy Crunch! Oh my goodness, they can't get enough of it!"

"It's like they're eating candy right out of my hand," I said to the camera.

At the end of the segment, the clipboard lady and the spiky-haired makeup girl, bustled into the studio.

"Madison," said the clipboard lady, "Our makeup genius, Margo, came up with a brilliant idea! We're going to use you to demonstrate our Beauty-Does-It Insta-Perm Hair-Curling Gel."

I needed to think fast. How was I going to make it back to that Product Room without getting caught? I had an idea.

"Sounds good," I told her. "But I really, really have to go to the bathroom." I hopped around a little bit, just to make the point clear.

"We don't have much time for that sort of thing around here. Hurry up, it's down the hall." She pointed to a door just beyond the Product Room.

Perfect.

I worried they'd follow me, but they got caught up in a conversation with Sarah about eating the dog food. I heard them go on and on about how "brilliant" it was.

As I sprinted toward the Product Room, I ran smack into Alan Stone.

"Where are you going in such a hurry?"

"Uh, the bathroom." Ugh. I hate to lie.

"Don't be too long. Because of you our phones are ringing off the hook. Merchandise is flying out of here. There's never been a shortage of unhappy people who call us when they need to be cheered up with a little TV shopping therapy, but this is definitely a new record!"

Shopping therapy? Unhappy people? Did that mean *Florida* was unhappy? Was that the reason she bought so much stuff she didn't need from the TV?

"Take it from me, kid. You're a goldmine around here. The audience is going nuts for you."

Nice to hear, but I was hoping I wasn't going to be making a career out of this. I needed to get back to Truth or Consequences. But I did have one question I had to ask.

"Mr. Stone? Did your son really throw birdseed on your carpet so the pigeons would fly into the house?"

He laughed out loud. "Are you kidding? I haven't seen him since last March. He lives with his mother out on the West Coast. I don't even own a vacuum cleaner. The cleaning people handle that. But it made a cute story—right?"

"Uh, yeah, real cute." But it wasn't true. I felt sorry for his son, having a father who made up embarrassing stories like that.

The second that Alan Stone turned and headed for Studio B I made sure the coast was clear. I opened the door to the Product Room, slipped inside and shut it quietly behind me.

Merchandise was piled everywhere. Computers, ladders, kitchen stuff, makeup, hair dryers, toys, vacuum cleaners, coats, dresses, exercise outfits, exercise equipment, and jewelry. This place would have been Florida's dream come true. Then I noticed TVs lined up on the far side of the room. I raced over and found the remote control for the MegaPix 6000!

I grabbed it and quickly pushed ENTER. Nothing. I tried the

purple button. Nothing. I pushed button after button, but I didn't budge. Then I remembered. When I was cleaning the drool off the purple button, I might have been holding down the ENTER button at the same time. So I pushed the purple and ENTER buttons at the same time.

Still nothing.

What was I supposed to do? Just then the door clicked open.

"Madison? Are you in here?" It was the clipboard lady. "It's five minutes until the hair curling segment."

I panicked. Then I saw it. A bright silver button that said RETURN. Return is exactly what I needed to do. I pushed it and the purple button together. Ping! My body went icy cold. My vision blurred. Tingly lightning sparked through me. I shut my eyes, and when I opened them I had popped like a cork right back into Florida's living room.

Chapter Ten

Okay, that was the freakiest thing that had happened to me *ever*. I would have pinched myself to make sure it was real, but I didn't have to, because I was still wearing the blue flowered dress.

The good news? It was the first time in four months and twenty-four days that I hadn't had a minute to think about my topsy-turvy new life.

The *Shop 'Til you Drop Channel* was still playing on the TV, and Sarah was holding up a bottle of Beauty-Does-It Insta-Perm Hair-Curling Gel. "Next time we'll demonstrate this on Madison, but right now? We're going to curl up the spiky hair of our Makeup Queen, Margo."

I hit the off button on the remote. I didn't want to see another shopping show as long as I lived.

The living room looked pretty much the way I'd left it. Except that the paper towel I'd used to dry up Leroy's slobber was in a million little pieces on the floor. While I was busy starring on the *Shop 'Til You Drop Channel*, Leroy must have passed the time practicing how to be a paper shredder.

Leroy. Where was that dog? I raced through the house calling his name. He was fast asleep on my bed, snuggling with a pile of my dirty socks.

The last thing I needed was to have Florida find Leroy inside her house. I nudged him awake and led him by his collar to the backyard.

As I chained him to his monitor, he hung his head and whimpered.

"It's just for a little while, boy. I'll unhook you again as soon as I can. Promise."

It was hot as blazes, so I filled his bowl with cold water, then scratched his tummy spot that made his back leg shake with happiness.

"Hello."

It was the crazy lady. She was standing on her back porch, bundled in layers. "I just made some pie, Madison," she said. "Would you like some?"

How did she know my name?

"Uh, sorry, I can't," I said. "Maybe another time."

Like maybe when pigs can fly.

I hurried back into the house and shut the door. Even though she hadn't done anything strange, I couldn't be too sure, so I flipped the lock just in case.

It was then that I noticed Florida's ceramic poodle collection. Leroy had knocked them all down like bowling pins. Quick as anything, I set them back up and was relieved that none of them had broken.

It wasn't a second too soon because Florida walked in. After what I'd just been through, I was totally happy to see her.

"Florida!" I ran over and gave her a big hug.

She patted my head and took a quick step back.

"What an unexpected and energetic little greeting, dear. Careful, you'll wrinkle my new blouse."

I blushed. "Sorry," I said. "It's been a really long day."

"You're telling me! I'm sure I designed at least a dozen flower arrangements. And every last one of them was drop-dead gorgeous. I do have quite the knack. What did you do today? I hope our crazy neighbor didn't bother you."

"Not really. But she *was* watching me in the backyard."

Florida shook her head. "Why am I not surprised?"

What was that supposed to mean?

Then Florida noticed the dress. "Well, I see you've decided to dress like a lady. Honey, I do declare it almost makes you look pretty."

Almost? Gee, thanks.

"That gives me an inspired idea," Florida said. "Follow me. We are going on a mission."

She grabbed her purse, and we were out the door.

Chapter Eleven

"Honey, it's time for a little beautification," she said as she parked her Cadillac on Main Street. "Let's buy you something truly divine."

"How about a new soccer ball?" I asked.

"Why on earth would you need that?"

"Your neighbor's dog popped mine."

"Young lady, we're on a mission to beautify you, not to encourage you to be a tomboy."

Too late. I already was a tomboy.

Florida pushed open the door to the So Sweet Boutique.

"We are here to perform a little makeover magic," she told the saleslady, who turned out to be my grandmother's best friend, Patsy. Patsy was a raven-haired version of Florida, down to her curls and high-heeled shoes.

Together Florida and Patsy pulled some of the most hideous clothes off the racks and hung them on hooks in the dressing room. I was surrounded by matching shorts outfits with ribbons and bows, frilly flowery skirts, and dresses with puffy sleeves. How old did they think I was? Four?

"You are going to look like a little angel in all these clothes!" Without asking, Patsy pulled the blue flowered dress over my head, revealing my T-shirt and soccer shorts.

"Why, this is an interesting little fashion statement," she said. Then she yanked off my t-shirt. I couldn't believe it. I was eleven, for crying out loud! I could feel my cheeks blush red.

"Oh my goodness, this is *perfection*." Florida held up a baby-pink puffy dress. "Your mother had one just like it."

My mother? Never in a zillion years would she have worn something like that.

"I don't really like it," I mumbled.

"Nonsense! Besides, how do you know unless you try it on?"

"Most little girls would just love, love, love this dress," Patsy chimed in. "It won't hurt to give it a whirl."

I gave up and gave in.

"Oh my!" Florida beamed. "Picture perfect!"

I stared in the mirror at my reflection. I resembled a jumbo baby-pink frosted cupcake. All I needed was a candle on my head.

"You are a true vision of beauty!" Florida said. "We'll take it!"

Really? Didn't *I* have anything to say about it? Then it came to me. If I'd found the nerve to talk to millions of people on live TV, I could speak up to my grandmother.

"I'm sorry, but I don't want it."

"Of course you do, honey. It's a much better look for you."

"It would be if I was a toddler in a beauty pageant."

"Once you get used to it, I think you'll simply love, love, love it," Patsy said.

"I doubt it," I said.

"Let's not be rude, Madison." Florida said through clenched teeth. "Why don't we put this dress aside for a minute and you can try on these other things?"

I swallowed hard. "I'm sorry, but I don't like any of these, so please don't waste your money because I won't wear them. Ever."

We left the store without buying a thing.

By the time we got home, Florida's eyeballs looked like they were going to shoot out of her head.

"Do you know how embarrassing it is that you behaved that way in front of Patsy? Go to your room! I want you to spend your time thinking long and hard about how ungrateful you are. And for all I care, you can stay there until Christmas!"

"Sorry I embarrassed you," I said before I stomped off. "But I'm not a baby doll!"

Then I slammed the door of my room.

Being stuck in a shopping show for the rest of my life suddenly seemed like an improvement over living with my grandmother.

I curled up on my bed with the photograph of my mom and me at the beach. I'd give anything if I could zap myself into it the way I did into the TV.

Even a hundred-to-one chance was better than nothing.

I dug the backup remote from my underwear drawer and scrambled back onto my bed. I positioned my fingers over the purple button and the ENTER button then aimed it straight at the photo. I held my breath and pushed.

Nothing.

I pressed the buttons again and again, but no matter how hard or how many times I did, there was only silence. No ping. No blurry vision. No icy feeling flowing through my veins. Only the feeling of tears sliding down my cheeks and the same old sadness that had been churning inside me for the past four months and twenty-four days.

I shoved the remote back in my drawer and peered out the window. A thick layer of clouds rolled in, turning the dusky blue sky licorice-black.

I curled up under my mom's ferry jacket and shut my eyes tight. Then the room exploded with a flash of light. A crash of thunder rattled the house. I heard Leroy howl. Then again: flash, boom, howl.

My mother once told me about how much she loved the sounds and smells of New Mexico summer thunderstorms when she was a kid. I inhaled deeply and took in the musky scent of laundry drying in the sun, mingled with the cinnamon and butterscotch jacket. The echoing sounds reminded me of the rhythm from an African dance I saw on a school field trip. Flash! Boom! Howl! Flash! Boom! Howl!

When the thunder crashed right after the lightning flashed I knew the storm was blowing closer. FlashBoom! Howl! FlashBoom! Howl! FlashBoom! FlashBoom! But where was the howl?

I heard a loud scraping against the house, which scared me stiff until I recognized Leroy's whimper. I opened the window and he sailed inside. He had worked off his chain. Leroy shook like a leaf and hid behind my legs.

"It's all right, boy." I slammed the window shut and hugged him tight.

FlashBoom! FlashBoom! FlashBoom!

We snuggled on the bed, even though he smelled like stinky feet. Together we listened to the sound of the sky opening up and pouring down rain.

That night I dreamed that Leroy and I zapped into *Just Jessica*. Carlee Knight, the girl who played kind, misunderstood movie star Jessica, invited us to come live with her in a beautiful white mansion high on a mountain.

When I awoke the next morning the sun was blazing. Apparently Leroy had gone on a midnight scavenger hunt. He was on my bed surrounded by my tennis shoes, a mountain of socks and underwear, and a pile of chewed pencils. He was busy devouring the ballerina lamp that he'd managed to fetch off the nightstand.

When I heard the blast of Florida's hair dryer I knew she was getting ready for work. It went silent and then there was a knock on my door.

"Honey, are you in there? Oh Mad-i-son!" She sounded awfully cheery, as if she'd forgotten all about our disastrous shopping expedition.

I pretended to be asleep. Besides, she *had* told me to stay in my room until Christmas.

I scratched Leroy's belly, and he licked my hand. I whispered to him that on the nights he was left chained in the yard, I'd let him in to sleep on my bed.

If only he didn't smell so bad. I decided that if Leroy was going to be my new roommate, I'd need to give him a bath.

Chapter Twelve

The second Florida slammed the front door I scrambled out of bed.

"Leroy, today we're on a mission to beautify you, but I promise I won't make you wear any cupcake dresses."

Leroy thumped his stumpy tail.

I knew I'd have no trouble finding shampoo in this house. I headed straight for the refrigerator. That's right. The refrigerator. There was barely a speck of food in there because it was filled to the brim with the beauty products Florida had bought from the shopping shows. Inside there were shampoos to make hair shinier, thicker, curlier, and straighter. I pulled out a bottle of *Triple Plump 'N Thick Miracle Shine* because on the bottle it said that it smelled of vanilla and mint. Vanilla and mint would be a huge improvement over stinky feet.

Leroy followed me out to the backyard. The scorching sun had already dried the ground after last night's rain. Big puffy picture-clouds crept across the wide blue sky. And over at the neighbor lady's house the curtains were pulled shut.

I turned on the hose and drenched Leroy from head to tail. I dumped the entire bottle of shampoo on his back and worked it through his fur into big frothy bubbles until he looked like he was covered in whipped cream.

The second he was rinsed off, he shook and sprayed me all over. I was almost as sopping wet as he was, but I didn't mind. Now we both smelled like vanilla and mint.

When he was dry Leroy looked like a different dog. The *Triple Plump 'N Thick Miracle Shine* shampoo made his fur as sparkly as starlight. It puffed him up big as a porcupine except that he felt super-soft. In fact, after the bath, Leroy looked cute.

I decided to sketch a picture of him and ran inside to get my drawing supplies. I told him to sit, and he remained still as a statue, not even scratching a single flea.

As I put the finishing touches on my Leroy sketch, the crazy lady's screen door creaked open. She carried a big yellow plastic basket of wet laundry.

"Well, somebody looks like a brand-new dog," she said as she pulled clothespins from her fanny pack and clipped a row of ratty sweaters, sweatpants, giant bras, and panties on the line.

"Is that your doing, Madison?"

I sure wished I knew how she knew my name.

I concentrated on my drawing pad in my lap, pretending I hadn't heard her. But from the corner of my eye I saw that she was staring straight at me. My heart pounded ka-thump, ka-thump, ka-thump. I was trapped.

"Sunshine!" Our back door opened wide and there was Grandpa Jack! I sailed into his arms so fast that my pencils and sketchbook went spinning into the dust.

"Grandpa!"

He scooped me up and hugged me close.

With Leroy at his heels, Grandpa carried me inside. We sank into the big corduroy easy chair in the corner of the living room, with me on his lap. I told Leroy to sit, and he curled up at our feet.

"Looks like you made yourself a friend," Grandpa said, patting Leroy on the head.

I snuggled into Grandpa's neck, and he smelled just like my mom always said he did. The same way he smelled on that horrible day back in February when he and Florida came to Violet's house. Spicy aftershave and fresh dirt. My grandpa was the mirror image of a bigger-than-life cowboy, right down to his bushy black moustache and soiled ten-gallon hat.

I sure wished Grandpa lived here with Florida instead of in a trailer two hours away near the White Sands Missile Range. That's where he worked fixing trucks.

"Life sure is tough sometimes, ain't it, Sunshine?" Grandpa said.

"Yeah." I really didn't want to talk about what had happened with my mom. Even with Grandpa. I didn't want my eyes to fill up like swimming pools.

"I want to show you somethin'." Grandpa Jack pulled out his wallet. Inside was a picture of my mom with my grandpa. She looked about fifteen. She wore a red bandana, a pair of torn jeans, and a Bart Simpson T-shirt. Around her neck was a silver chain with a red charm that was too tiny to make out.

Grandpa wiped away a tear with the back of his hand. A sad smile curled up his lips. "See? My little girl's still with me every single day."

We contemplated the picture in silence.

I wished a picture was enough for me but it never would be. My mom wasn't with me every day. She was gone. Sometimes the only way I could make sense of it all was to pretend. Lately I imagined she was away on an extended vacation someplace exotic, and she'd be picking me up any day. Dumb, I know.

Grandpa tucked away the photo. He pulled out a tangle of keys. "Well, Sunshine, today your ol' Grandpa Jack is on a mission."

Chapter Thirteen

"I thought missions were Florida's thing," I said to Grandpa.

"Originally they were, so I had to come up with my own mission to thwart some of her missions."

Going against my grandmother? That sounded like Mission Impossible to me.

"Our mission this mornin', Sunshine, is to load up my truck with boxes of unopened junk that your grandma keeps buying. Then we're gonna sell it down at the flea market. Are you in?"

"Sure, but won't she notice they're gone?"

"She ain't figured it out yet. She's got so much dang stuff, she never misses a truckload of boxes. This way I get back some of the money she's spent on all this garbage."

Before we packed Grandpa's truck and before I tied Leroy back up, I checked to see if the neighbor lady was still in the yard. The coast was clear.

Leroy whimpered when I clipped on his chain so I told him he could sleep with me that night on my bed. I gathered up my pencils and sketchpad.

When I was back inside, I heard the bang of the screen door. Through the window I spied the neighbor lady marching right up to Leroy. She unzipped her fanny pack and pulled out an enormous meaty bone. He snatched it and thumped his tail. Okay, maybe she *seemed* nice enough, but it didn't mean she wasn't a weirdo.

Out in the garage we were met with stacks and stacks of unopened boxes. Together we carried the piles from the far corner and loaded them into Grandpa's old red pickup. He said those were the ones that had been there the longest. Then I helped him shove another stack into the area we'd just emptied.

"Those are for next time."

Clearly Grandpa Jack had a system.

During the drive down to Las Cruces, Grandpa played Country/Western music on his CD player, and he taught me the words. By the time we made it to the flea market, I'd learned three songs:

"I'm Just a Bug on the Windshield of Life."

"My Head Hurts, My Feet Stink, And I Don't Love You."

"I've Been Flushed From the Bathroom Of Your Heart."

We pulled into Big Daddy's Flea Market just before noon. You could spot the place from way down the highway because there was a humongous statue of a guy with a black moustache holding up a "Big Daddy" sign. He was at least thirty feet tall, and looked exactly like a giant younger version of Grandpa Jack.

The flea market was jam-packed with people selling and buying all kinds of junk. Old toys, old tools, old clothes, and old VHS movies for fifty cents apiece.

"Most of these folks get here at sunrise. But not us. Florida's stuff flies out of here in a jiffy since it's all brand spankin' new."

And boy, was he right. You would have thought we'd brought rare and ancient treasures the way people swarmed us. Grandpa zipped open boxes with a hunting knife, and I helped pull things out. People bargained for items even before I could set them on the table. We sold one fake-fur vest, two sets of dishes, three hair dryers, four designer purses, five silver watches, and six sparkly cocktail rings before I gave up counting.

By three o'clock everything was gone. We made almost $2,000, so we celebrated and bought shredded beef tacos from Romero's Taco

Truck. Then we headed back to Truth or Consequences.

"You're a dandy business partner, Sunshine. How 'bout we make this a standin' date? Two Saturdays a month. Your grandma heads to the flower shop, and we conduct a little business." He rummaged in his pocket and pulled out a toothpick to dig leftover beef taco from his teeth.

"Okay." I liked the idea of spending time with Grandpa Jack.

"Oh—and let's just keep this whole business deal between you and me."

That felt a little sneaky to me. It was almost a lie.

"What if Florida finds out?"

Grandpa snorted. "I've been at this for fourteen years. Twice a month, spring through summer. She ain't caught on yet."

Wow. Fourteen years. I was minus three years old when he started selling off my grandmother's things.

"But it *is* Florida's stuff. Are you sure it's okay that we sell it without telling her?"

"Let me ask you this. Is it okay that she wastes my money on all this garbage?"

"I guess not. It does seem a little flaky."

Grandpa let out a long whistle. "Flaky as a biscuit. That woman has a big ol' serious problem."

Maybe Grandpa Jack was right about that. And she sure seemed to need a whole lot of shopping therapy to deal with it.

"Oh—and you deserve a little something for all your hard work." He pulled out a fat wad of cash, peeled off a twenty-dollar bill and handed it to me.

I thanked him and slipped the twenty into my pocket. But I couldn't shake the feeling that maybe what we did wasn't 100 percent right.

"Now are you ready to learn another Country/Western song?"

"You bet."

So we sang "Queen of My Doublewide Trailer" all the way home.

Chapter Fourteen

The second we pulled up to the house, Florida sashayed out the front door in a fire-engine-red mini-dress, as if she were going to some super-fancy dinner party.

"Welcome home, Jack!" In her spiky high heels, she teetered into Grandpa's open arms.

"If it ain't my sweetie-pie cupcake!" Grandpa scooped her right off the ground.

They seemed really happy to see each other.

Inside the house, the dining room table was set with shiny silverware and gold-rimmed china. It was lit by candlelight even though the sun hadn't gone down. Soft music played on the stereo. And the TV was off.

"Jack, darling, while I get busy in the kitchen, could you wash my car? Pretty please, with a bright-red cherry on top?"

"Will do, Cupcake."

I followed Grandpa and he got to work sponging the desert dust off Florida's Cadillac.

"How 'bout giving me a hand, Sunshine?"

As we scoured the gold metal until it gleamed, I got to thinking. "Grandpa, could I come live with you in Alamogordo?"

He stopped scrubbing and his eyes got misty.

"Sunshine, Alamogordo's no place for you. My *life's* no place for you. Your ol' grandpa's up at the crack of dawn, fixin' every broken-down machine at the Missile Range. Sometimes I don't roll back in until the wee hours of the mornin'. Here's the truth, plain and simple, though you may not appreciate hearing it. Your mom had to grow up with Florida, and now you do too."

I fought back tears as I wiped the windshield dry.

"Mad-i-son!" Florida yelled from inside the house. "I could use a little help in here. Pronto!"

Grandpa shrugged. "Better go."

I sighed. Seven more years of this until I could move away to college. I considered drawing a calendar and crossing off the days.

I expected to see my grandmother in a whirlwind of food preparation, but her arctic white kitchen was spotless.

"Let's get dinner on the table." She opened the oven, pulled out a foil-lined bag and slid a meatloaf onto a serving dish.

"A little something I picked up at the deli counter at the Bullock's Shur-Sav. Your Grandpa Jack believes it's my home-cooked specialty. So honey, let's not tell him it's store-bought. It'll be a little secret between us girls."

There sure seemed to be a lot of secrets between these two.

I dropped the bag in the trash while Florida heated a container of mashed potatoes from the market. Then she microwaved frozen peas and dumped them in a bowl.

By the time we carried the food into the dining room, Grandpa Jack was sitting at the table.

"Sunshine, your grandmother makes the finest meatloaf in the entire state of New Mexico." He helped himself to the fattest slice.

Florida kissed the top of his head. "You big old sweet-talking flatterer, Jack. It was just a little something I whipped up."

I took a bite. I had to admit the meatloaf from the market tasted delicious.

Florida picked at her meal. "So Madison, what mischief did you and your grandpa get into today?"

What was I supposed to say? I shot a glance at Grandpa Jack, hoping he'd save me.

He didn't skip a beat. "We went out and about. You can't keep a child cooped up in this godforsaken town for long. A young girl needs to see the world!"

"Grandpa taught me some funny songs," I volunteered.

"Did he now? How about singing one for me? Grandpa knows the most amusing songs."

I sang a verse from "Queen of My Doublewide Trailer":

So I made her the queen of my doublewide trailer
With the polyester curtains and the redwood deck;
Times she's run off and I've got to trail her –
Dang her black heart and her pretty red neck.

Florida's jaw clenched up. "That's enough, young lady. Stop it this instant."

So I did. Grandpa looked guilty.

"Your grandpa knows how I feel about that wretched song. He had no business teaching it to you. Maybe I should teach you a little ditty about a woman who would never in this lifetime move into her husband's teeny-tiny doublewide trailer way off in nowheresville Alamogordo."

Wow. And I thought it was just a silly song.

"For Pete's sake, Florida, do you have to drag her into this?"

"You taught her the song Jack, not me. I don't care how many times you ask. I'm never moving into that trailer with you." Florida stared at him with steely eyes.

"I'm not asking. I was all done asking years ago. I was only teaching her a song!" He dropped his head in his hands like he had a headache.

"I don't believe you for a minute, Jack Brown, so don't you lie to me!"

I could see Grandpa was fed up. "We're over and done with this conversation, Florida. I'm goin' to watch some TV. The baseball game is on."

"There's a special on the *Beauty Channel* tonight I'm planning to watch," Florida said through her gritted teeth.

Things between them were so tense I thought I'd try to help out the situation. "With Florida's new picture-in-a-picture TV you can watch both of your shows at the same time," I told Grandpa, trying to sound as cheerful as possible.

Grandpa's face turned beet-red. "For criminy sakes, Florida! When did you go and buy a new TV? Is that any way to spend my hard-earned money?"

"For your information, it didn't cost a thing. Besides, it's my money too. I make some at the flower shop, and my daddy left me plenty when he died. I can spend it however I please, Mr. Jack Tightwad Brown."

"You make chicken feed arranging those flowers, and your Daddy's money has been gone for over *eight years*, Florida," Grandpa yelled. "And you've burned it up in a big ol' bonfire of junk!"

"I don't believe you, Jack. You're just saying that, and I don't have to listen because I'm leaving!" Florida grabbed her purse and bolted for the door.

"Not before I do!" Grandpa ran out ahead of her. "I've had enough of this," he shouted. "I'm going back to Alamogordo!" Outside, he slammed the door of his pick-up.

His truck started up, then her Cadillac. They gunned them in opposite directions down the street.

Grandpa Jack and Florida were the Duke and Duchess of Bickering. My mom barely ever raised her voice. Maybe since she grew up watching my grandparents' fights she figured there was a better way to be. I wished she had been there to tell them to cut it out.

I cleaned the kitchen and went into my room. There was a postcard of a French bakery on my bed. It was from Violet.

Dear Madison,

Greetings from Paris! Today my grandma took me on a tour of a real French bakery. The chef taught us how to make apple tarts. I'm having the best time ever, but I miss you so much!

Avec amour (that means "with love" in French),
Violet

I missed Violet too—more than she could ever imagine. It didn't seem fair that she was in Paris with her perfect grandmother, and I was left all alone in some dusty out-in-the-middle-of-nowhere town, living with my totally imperfect grandmother.

I peered through my bedroom window into the dusky yard. Leroy wasn't in his usual spot. Maybe the greasy-haired guy had brought him in for the night, since now he smelled more like chewing gum than like a dirty dog. I listened to crickets chirping in the backyard. A pack of coyotes howled in the distance.

And me? I sat on my bed all alone with no one to talk to and nothing to do. I kept thinking about Violet, her awesome summer in Paris, and my lonely new life in Truth or Consequences, New Mexico.

Then I realized it was Saturday night and I had the power to do something even more extraordinary than Violet. I went into the living room and turned on the MegaPix 6000.

I was going to zap myself into an episode of *Just Jessica*.

Chapter Fifteen

When I switched on the MegaPix, the *Just Jessica* theme song was beginning, and my heart got jumpy. I took a super-deep breath, then pushed the purple button and the ENTER button at the same time. Ping! The purple question mark and those familiar words popped on the screen.

Are you SURE you want to choose this channel?
If "yes" push ENTER again.

Was I sure? I was absolutely, positively 100 percent sure.

I pushed ENTER. Ping! Everything blurred. Cold tingles rocketed through my body.

When I opened my eyes I was standing on the set of *Just Jessica*. This was going to be way better than being cooped up at Florida's all by myself on a Saturday night.

"Where have you been, Madison? They're waiting for you in makeup." A lady scurried over. She was super-short and round, with hair so curly it looked as if she had miniature Slinkies popping out all over her head.

"The name's Martha. I'm your kid wrangler. My job is to stick with you. Your job is to listen to everything I say." She talked a mile a minute. "Glad you're here. I had a panicky moment when I thought you were a no-show."

Wow. She'd been expecting me? Just like the people on the shopping show? It was so confusing. Did the MegaPix send secret signals? Or a text message? Or was it my destiny to push those buttons and this was *supposed* to be happening? I sure wished I knew how all this magic stuff worked.

Martha took off. I had to run to keep up with her. If she were on roller blades, I don't think she could have moved any faster. I slid the remote control safely inside my pocket.

Everywhere I looked, people were setting up lights, pulling long cables, and rolling cameras on dollies. I chased behind Martha, keeping an eagle-eye lookout for the show's stars, Carlee Knight and Jamal Jackson—the boy who played Curtis. They were nowhere in sight.

In the makeup room Martha sat me down on a high swivel chair. A lady with a bunch of ear piercings aimed a silvery metal pen contraption at my face.

"Makeup time. Close your eyes. Don't breathe," she said.

I gulped air and shut my eyes. Then came a hissing sound and the cold sting of stinky goop airbrushed on my face. This was way weirder than what they'd done on the shopping show. Between holding my breath and the wet cloud of makeup tickling my nostrils, my lungs were ready to explode.

"Okay. Breathe."

Not a second too soon. I exhaled hard and opened my eyes. I didn't look like me anymore. I looked as fake as a porcelain doll.

"Don't worry. Looks ridiculous in person, but on camera you'll look great," said Martha.

We headed for the wardrobe department where a lady named Shannon handed me purple leggings and a flowery turquoise sweatshirt. The first thing I noticed was the kangaroo pocket in the sweatshirt. Score! It was the perfect size to hide my remote control. Not that I wanted to zap out of there any time soon, but I definitely didn't want to lose track of that remote again.

"Thirty minutes before you're needed on set. Do you want to look over your script, or do you have everything memorized?"

Memorized? I didn't even know who in the heck I was supposed to be in this show. "It wouldn't hurt to take a look," I said.

She handed me a script and I settled into a big comfy chair in the corner of the room and began to read.

The script was called *Sweet Fourteen*. Across every page in faded gray print it said *Madison McGee*. They'd printed this script just for me! It was the strangest thing ever to know they'd been expecting me all along.

On the first page was a list of the characters. Next to my name it said *Sophie—Ashley's young bratty cousin*. Ashley? The nastiest character on the show? Oh great.

I read as fast as I could. In the script, Ashley was throwing a fancy fourteenth birthday party and didn't want to invite Jessica and her best friend, Curtis. But Sophie was a huge fan and threatened to blackmail Ashley if she didn't invite them. Ashley finally gave in, but just to be mean, she told Jessica and Curtis that it was a crazy-pajama party.

On the day of the party, Jessica and Curtis showed up wearing their PJs. Near the end of the script, Ashley tripped on her super-spiky high heels and knocked Sophie into the swimming pool. Because Sophie couldn't swim, Jessica and the boy at the party she had a crush on saved her. In the end, the boy asked Jessica out on a date, but she couldn't go because she had to shoot a movie.

Here's the first thing I thought: I was really glad I knew how to swim.

The second thing? I would be going to a "party" with the entire cast of *Just Jessica*. And Carlee Knight would be "saving" me from fake drowning in a swimming pool. I was pretty sure this would be the best day of my life!

I read my lines twice more. I don't know if it was the magic or my memory, but I knew every single word I was supposed to say.

When it was time to shoot my first scene, Martha and I snaked through a maze of gigantic buildings, each one as big as a Wal-Mart. I was worried about meeting Allison Hunter, who played Ashley. In a matter of seconds, I was going to be face-to-face with the worst mean girl ever.

Martha stopped in front of a heavy gray door and yanked it open. A sign on the building said: SOUND STAGE 4.

Here goes nothing, I thought.

Chapter Sixteen

The first person I saw when I walked through the door? Mean Girl Allison Hunter.

"Hey! You must be Madison!" she said.

I was speechless.

"Or should I just call you, 'Cousin'? Anyway, nice to meet you." She grinned and stuck her hand straight out, so I shook it.

"Nice to meet you too," I mumbled, maybe because I was in a state of shock. Allison Hunter didn't seem to be mean. In fact, she seemed kind of nice.

"Don't worry, I don't bite. Everyone who meets me for the first time thinks I'm just like my character Ashley—a first class, stuck-up pain-in-the-butt. That's if they watch the show. Do you watch it?"

"I've seen it," I said. "Actually every episode."

"And now you'll be in one. How cool is that? Been in the business for long?" As she talked, she stretched and bent and popped up and down on her toes.

"Not really. I was on a shopping show once."

"Awesome! You gotta start somewhere!"

We shot the first two scenes on a set I'd seen at least a million times before. It was Ashley's rich-girl bedroom. There was a motorized TV screen that dropped down from the ceiling with the push of a button, a fancy gilded bed that some real French princess had slept in back in the

15th century, and a closet almost as big as Florida's whole living room.

The first thing we shot was the scene when Sophie arrives at Ashley's house. I have to admit—at first I stank. I was terrible with a capital "T." In the scene, Ashley was on her cell phone and didn't want to be interrupted. I was supposed to be a holy terror and interrupt her anyway.

"I'm more important than any dumb phone call," I said.

"Cut!" yelled the director. "Move in closer to her. And Madison? I want it louder and brattier!"

I tried my line again. *"I'm more important than any dumb phone call."*

"Cut! That's all you've got? Make it 100 percent brattier."

I tried it again and again and again. By the time he told me to make it 1,000 percent brattier, my eyes stung with tears.

Allison leaned over and whispered, "Think of the brattiest kid you've ever known."

Easy.

"Molly Cooper," I said. We'd been in fifth grade together. She always said mean things about her friends and worse things about her enemies. She whined about everything.

"Pretend you're Molly Cooper," Ashley said.

So I did. I acted exactly like Molly Cooper, and the director loved it.

"Now that's what I call acting!" he said. "Cut and we're moving on!"

He was so happy that he kissed me smack on top of my head.

The girls who played the twins, Tiffany and Tanya, came in for the next scene and sat with Allison up on the huge fancy princess bed.

The director told me to lie on the floor and pretend to be drawing a picture of Allison and a boy named Dylan. He was the kid in the script that both Ashley and Jessica had crushes on. The director said I didn't have to draw for real because they'd hired an artist who'd already done the picture I was going to show the girls. I was supposed to hold up the artist's finished drawing and tell Allison that if she didn't invite Jessica,

I would give the picture to Dylan at the party. Basic blackmail.

But the prop guy had forgotten all about getting someone to do the drawing, so I volunteered to do it myself.

"I'm a much better artist than I am an actress," I promised the director. So he let me.

Okay, this may be lame, but getting to sketch that picture was one of the coolest parts of my whole day. Why? My drawing was going to be on national television! Some people might think it was way cooler that *I* got to be on television, but my lifelong dream is to be an artist, not an actress.

I really wished my mom could have seen it. She'd always told me that someday millions of people would see my artwork, and I'd be famous. She couldn't have imagined it would happen quite this way. But who could?

While the three girls said their lines, I started in on my sketch.

When we got to the blackmail part of the scene, I said my line in my brattiest, whiniest, most Molly Cooper voice: *"But I love Jessica. I've seen all her movies. If you don't invite her I—I—I'm going to show your little lover boy Dylan THIS when he comes to the party—and you can't stop me!"*

Then I held up my drawing. In it Allison had her hands clasped to her chest. Dozens of hearts flowed from her, knocking over the terrified boy. Allison's speech bubble said, "Marry me, Dylan!!!" A thought bubble over the boy said, "Mommy! Helllllp!!!"

The girls burst into laughter. They weren't supposed to, but they did. They told me they didn't know what was funnier, the picture I'd drawn or the way I'd said my line.

The director yelled, "Cut," and asked me to do exactly what I'd done before. He told the other girls to try to keep a straight face. We started again.

Every time I said my line, the girls cracked up. By the fourth take I was laughing right along with them. You know how sometimes you start laughing at something and then after a while you're just laughing at yourself laughing? That's what happened. Even the director was in hysterics. It took us fifteen takes to get it right.

The director breathed a sigh of relief and chuckled. "Well, at least we have some good footage for the blooper reel."

Chapter Seventeen

By the time we were ready to shoot the party scene, I could barely keep my eyes open. When I'd zapped into the TV it was already eight at night in Truth or Consequences, and it felt as if I'd been on the *Just Jessica* set for *hours*. It sure took a lot longer to make a TV show than it did to watch one. I wondered if I'd traveled backwards in time to film the show, and then when I zapped out again I'd be back in real time. It made my head hurt just thinking about it.

I changed into a fancy velvet party dress I'm sure Florida would have loved, slipped my remote control into a matching purse, and hurried outside behind Martha. An enormous bus waited to take us to where we'd be shooting the party scene.

That's when my second wind kicked in. At last I was going to meet Carlee and Jamal!

The bus was packed with kids who were playing the party guests. Allison waved me over. She'd saved me the last open seat.

Martha sat in the only spot left, on the step at the front of the bus.

"There's no room for Carlee and Jamal," I pointed out to Allison.

"Jamal's up front." She nodded toward a dark-skinned boy with glasses. His nose was buried in a book and his signature short, spiky dreadlocks were hidden beneath a grey knit ski cap. I couldn't believe I'd walked right past him and hadn't even noticed.

"The guy's a total bookworm. Mostly he keeps to himself, but that's cool. His mom forced him into show business. The minute he turns eighteen he'll quit and tell his parents to go to you-know-where. He wants to go to college. I'll bet you someday he finds a cure for cancer or something. He's a complete brainiac."

"What about Carlee?"

"Carlee? Oh, you'll meet her on location."

We drove from the film studio into the town of Bel Air. It was one of the fanciest neighborhoods in Los Angeles, right up there with Beverly Hills. The bus pulled in front of an enormous mansion—the place where Allison's character Ashley was throwing her Sweet Fourteen party. Everyone filed into the backyard. I couldn't believe my eyes. Surrounding a humongous swimming pool were life-sized Greek statues. There were so many exotic potted plants blooming with giant jungle flowers I had to remind myself we hadn't just parachuted into a super-ritzy South Sea Islands resort.

The director got busy, telling everyone where to stand.

At first I was supposed to sit on a marble bench and look bored. Allison and her TV friends hung out by the pool with the boy playing the part of Dylan. I have to admit he was kind of cute—and I don't even really like boys that way.

Then I finally saw her. Carlee Knight. She and Jamal were dressed in silly black-and-white spotted Dalmatian footy pajamas. They were just inside the house, getting ready for their entrance. I smiled my friendliest smile but I don't think she saw me, which was okay. It was almost time for our first big scene together.

The cameras rolled, and Carlee and Jamal walked into the backyard. Everyone playing the party guests acted super-rude and chanted, "Ew, ew! It's P.U. LePew!"

I was supposed to look star-struck. When we were done with the scene, the director complimented me. He said I did it exactly right. The truth? I hadn't been acting. I *was* star-struck.

Finally it was the time I'd been waiting for—my first scene with Carlee Knight. The director told me to push and shove through the crowd of kids to get to her. On the way I needed to snatch a paper plate from the food table so she could sign her autograph on it.

"Action!" he yelled.

I jumped up and did what I was told. Push, shove, push, shove, grab the paper plate. When I got to Carlee Knight, I was shaking on the inside, but I was determined not to show it on the outside. I didn't want to make a fool of myself. I stuck straight to the script and said my lines.

"Ignore them. They're mean. I'm Ashley's cousin, Sophie. Don't hold that against me, okay?" I held out my hand for her to shake, just the way it said to in the script.

"I won't." She shook my hand and smiled bright as a billion birthday candles.

"I'm a huge fan," I gushed. *"Could I have your autograph?"* I held out the plate.

"Of course. Anything for a fan." She fished inside her purse, pulled out a pen and signed:

"Your friend, Jessica LaPew."

"Gosh, thanks," I gushed again, just like I was supposed to. *"I'll never ever eat a single crumb off this plate."*

Carlee laughed, her white teeth flashing bright as her smile.

"Cut! Perfect! We're moving on!" Wow. One take. Of course, Carlee was perfect. As for me, I guess I did okay because I'd barely been acting.

She turned to walk back inside the house. I worked up the nerve to talk to her for real, with no script involved.

"Excuse me, Carlee—"

She spun around and stared. I was instantly tongue-tied.

"Well?" she asked.

At last I spit it out. "Uh, my real name is Madison McGee, but I actually am a true fan. In real life, I mean."

"Oh."

"Would you mind signing your real autograph on a plate? One for me, and one for my best friend, Violet?"

"Sorry, Madeline or whatever your name is. I don't do autographs on set. Contact my fan club. Or maybe you can buy one on eBay." She turned and disappeared inside the house.

Seriously? My whole world practically crumbled on the spot. Carlee Knight, the star who played nice girl Jessica LaPew, was *mean*. I didn't know how I was ever going to break it to Violet.

I felt a hand on my shoulder. It was Allison.

"Don't let her get to you, Madison. The girl has issues. She may be pretty and talented, but you know how many real friends Carlee has? None. I used to hate her. Now I just feel sorry for her. Carlee Knight is not a happy person."

Boy, was that an understatement!

Chapter Eighteen

I spent the rest of the afternoon trying to figure out what it would take to get Carlee Knight to understand that life would be way more fun if she was nice to people. My mom always said if you treat unkind people with kindness, it's possible they'll eventually come around.

So my mission was to be super-nice to Carlee Knight even if she had been super-mean to me. By the end of the day I was pretty sure my niceness would overwhelm her and she'd start treating everyone with kindness.

It didn't quite work out that way.

"Want a bite of my chocolate cake?" I'd asked her when we took a break for lunch.

"You think I'd eat the same crap the catering company serves you? I have my own gourmet lunch brought in. And about that chocolate cake? It will make you fat."

I thought that was extremely rude, but I kept on with my mission.

Later I tried to make conversation with her. My mom had always said a lot of people like to talk about themselves.

"What's your favorite part about being on TV?" I asked.

"Why would I tell you?" Carlee snapped.

Oh boy. This was going to be harder than I'd imagined.

When it was time to have our makeup retouched, the lady with the multiple ear piercings had only just started on me with that airbrush business when Carlee stomped over in a huff.

"Can't you people get this blush on evenly? Honestly!"

Okay—the weirdest thing? She sounded just like whiny Molly Cooper.

I hopped off the chair and let Carlee take my place. The makeup lady said, "Thank you." And you know what Carlee said? Absolutely positively nothing.

The rest of the afternoon I smiled at Carlee Knight at least twelve times. And here's how many times she smiled back at me: zero.

Finally it was time to shoot my big falling-in-the-pool scene. Cameras were set up everywhere. There was even one under the water. I ditched my remote control behind the marble bench so it wouldn't get wet when I was "accidentally" pushed into the swimming pool.

By now I wasn't nearly so excited about being "saved" by Carlee Knight. I just wanted to get the whole thing over with.

I stood on my mark near the edge of the pool, and the director called, "Action!" The boy who played Dylan flirted with Tiffany. Allison teetered in between them on her spiky heels. She stumbled into Tiffany, who bumped into Dylan, who tripped back into Allison. Allison fell onto her butt and knocked me into the pool. It made me think of that game Mousetrap where one thing falls, then another and another, until finally you catch the mouse. I guess first I was the mousetrap, and then I was the mouse.

I waved my arms frantically, pretending to drown. Right on cue, Carlee and the boy who played Dylan jumped into the pool to save me. They dragged me to the steps. As I coughed up water, they kept asking if I was okay.

When the cameras were rolling, Carlee was just the way I'd imagined her to be in real life. Someone who could easily be your best friend. In our scene she draped her arm around my shoulder, and she was kind. But it was just an act. Besides, I already had a true best friend, even though now I lived more than a thousand miles away from her, and she was spending the summer in Paris.

As soon as the director yelled, "Cut!" Carlee let go of me as if I had some deadly disease.

"Thank God that's over," she said. "I despise getting wet."

She stood up so fast she knocked me sideways, and I smacked my right arm on the edge of the concrete pool. Hard. I knew it was an accident, but it hurt like heck. I cried out in pain.

"Don't be such a baby. Maybe we should get Wardrobe to bring you a diaper," she snapped. Then she walked away. That was the last thing Carlee Knight ever said to me.

While they shot the scene where Dylan asks Jessica out on a date, I retrieved my remote control. Martha brought me my own clothes and led me into a room in the house so I could get changed.

When I was dressed and dry I looked out the window and watched Carlee Knight climb into a shiny black limousine. Of course. That's why she wasn't on the bus!

You might think it was nuts to imagine that my Carlee Knight kindness mission would work, but maybe I just didn't have enough time. I needed more than half a day to show Carlee Knight that in the long run it pays to be nice.

Martha kept bugging me to hurry because it was time to head back to the studio. That was the last place I wanted to go. I decided to try the old bathroom trick again.

This time I really went into the bathroom, locked the door and pulled out the remote control. I was sorry I wouldn't have a chance to say goodbye to Allison, but there wasn't much I could do. It was time to return to my regular old life in Truth or Consequences.

I pushed the purple button and the silver return button at the same time. Ping! Next thing I knew, I was standing back in Florida's living room and watching the credits roll by on the MegaPix. That's when I saw my name:

And introducing Madison McGee as Sophie.

I dropped the remote on the coffee table and checked the clock. It was only eight-thirty. I felt as if I'd been gone at least 100 hours, but I'd only zapped into the TV a half-hour before. My eyelids were heavy as bricks. My hair was damp and my arm ached. I headed into my room and opened my window wide in case Leroy wanted to come in.

I'm pretty sure I hadn't gone to bed at eight-thirty since I was in the second grade.

But that night I made an exception.

Chapter Nineteen

If you think zapping into the TV is freaky, the dream I had was even freakier. In my dream, or should I say my nightmare, Carlee Knight flushed my remote control down a toilet as big as a swimming pool, and I had to be on *Just Jessica* for the rest of my life. She forced me to bring her racks and racks of frilly pink clothes to try on. When I attempted to escape, she shoved me into the giant toilet. Just as she flushed, I woke up.

Through the haze of my dream I'd heard a strange sound coming from the backyard. A yowling sickly cat? A deranged coyote? The morning light streamed through the open window, but before I could look outside, Leroy joined in the chorus, howling at the top of his lungs. He was stretched out at the end of my bed.

"Shush!" I whispered as I clamped my hand over his muzzle.

If Florida caught Leroy in the house she'd have a first-class trophy-winning fit.

I slid out of bed and grabbed him by the collar. That's when I felt my arm. It hurt like heck. A gigantic plum purple bruise streaked from my shoulder down to my elbow.

"Ouch!" I let go of his collar to inspect the damage. Leroy licked my arm.

I cried out in pain. Maybe he was trying to help, but a hard dog lick on a giant bruise does not feel good.

When I peeked down the hallway the coast was clear. A concert of snores echoed from Florida's bedroom. Grandpa Jack must have changed his mind about going back to Alamogordo. Leroy kept trying to howl along to the backyard racket, so I held on to his muzzle until we were outside.

The second I let go he bolted next door, right over to the neighbor lady who was planting flowers and crooning at the top of her lungs.

Leroy howled in unison.

"Oh Leroy, you silly old dog. Is my singing that bad? It can't be much worse than the nutty racket you're making."

She had a point. Her singing and Leroy's howls seemed to be competing for Worst Noise Pollution Ever.

"What do you think?" she smiled. "Who's today's winner of the bad singing contest? Me or Leroy?"

Should I even talk to her? She *looked* friendly enough. Why did Florida think she was crazy, anyway? Leroy seemed to like her, and dogs usually have a sixth sense about those things. Before I could answer, she noticed my battered arm.

"Oh my goodness!" she said. "What happened?"

"An accident," I mumbled. I wasn't ready to tell anyone about *Just Jessica* and the magic TV.

"Come inside. We'll get you fixed up."

I hesitated, frozen to the spot. But after all I'd just been through, something dawned on me like one of those cartoon light bulbs that pop on over a character's head. Judging a person by their layers of clothes— or an actress by the character she plays on TV—wasn't too different than judging a book by its cover. I decided to take a chance. Leroy and I followed her up her back stairs and into the house.

"I'm sure your Grandma Florida calls me 'the crazy lady,' but let me properly introduce myself. I'm Rosalie Claire Kennedy."

"I'm Madison McGee."

"Yes, I know that. And it's a pleasure to finally meet you. Officially, that is."

I really wanted to know how she knew my name, but I was too nervous to ask.

We sat at the table in her sunny yellow kitchen and she had me rest my arm on a towel she spread on the Formica top. I told Leroy to sit. He did and then curled up by my feet.

Rosalie Claire unzipped her fanny pack, and I stared in amazement as she pulled out more stuff than could possibly fit in there: washcloths, rolls of gauze, tins, tubes, jars of mustard and honey, and a plump brown-skinned onion. It reminded me of Mary Poppins's carpetbag, only this was real.

Was it magic too?

My mom had always insisted there was no such thing as magic, and at one time I hadn't believed in it either. But after zapping into the TV, I now believed in magic 100 percent.

Rosalie Claire pulled a big ceramic bowl from her cupboard and got to work.

"So what's your story, Miss Madison? What brings you to Truth or Consequences?" she asked as she concocted a potion of mustard seed, honey, and smashed-up onion.

I wished I had that little printed card about my mom to pull out. I really didn't want to talk about it.

"What I mean is, what do you think life is going to deliver to you while you're here?"

That wasn't the question I'd expected at all. I had no idea, so I said the first thing that came to mind. "I guess I'll just go to school and wait to grow up so I can move away and go to college." But I couldn't picture myself going to the windowless school on the edge of town. Or finding friends here who would ever like me the way Violet did.

"And that's it? Really?" she asked, looking right into me with her brown-sugar eyes.

"My mom died. This is the only place I had to go." I stared down at my arm as she slathered it with sticky yellow mush. It resembled a jumbo hot dog with extra mustard.

Rosalie Claire's eyes brimmed with tears. "When I heard about your mama, it made me feel sad down to the bottom of my soul." She began to say something else, but she stopped herself and waved her words away.

"Madison," she finally said, "you can't be more than eleven. That's a lot of years of waiting around to leave a place. A lot of years of lost adventures. Pardon me for saying so, but that almost makes me sadder than your mama dying."

Leroy whimpered from under the table, as if he understood every word.

My eyes stung hot with tears. I could have kicked myself because I knew that talking about my mom would make me cry.

By the time Rosalie Claire had wrapped my arm up with a fat roll of snow-white gauze, I'd told Rosalie Claire things I'd never breathed to another soul. Not even Violet. All about my mom and her broken-down heart. All about not budging from the end of her hospital bed for two days straight when she was hooked up to monitors and tubes. All about watching her die. I told her about living with Violet until school was out. And I confessed that I absolutely, positively hated living with Florida.

Rosalie Claire's eyes were wet with tears too. "Life hasn't done you any favors lately. But remember—sometimes even when you think you hate something, life can jump out and surprise you. Sometimes things that seem bad can, in the end, turn out good. Truth or Consequences is a strange little town, but it can deliver up some big magic if you know how to look for it."

Magic, huh? I swallowed hard. "I think maybe I've found it. The magic, I mean," I confessed. Then I told her all about zapping into the TV.

"I've experienced my fair share of strange happenings in this world—and even some magic now and then—but this takes the cake," she said when I'd finished my story. "Thank goodness you figured out how to get back." She wrapped her cool hands around mine and clasped them tight.

"I don't think I'll do it again," I said. "Not after what happened with Carlee Knight. Although maybe it's better than sitting around and feeling sorry for myself half the time."

"I'm not so sure about that. When you take chances with deep powerful magic it can put you in some serious danger—even worse than this bruise. Not saying it *will*, but it can. At least you have Leroy to keep you company."

Leroy thumped his tail.

After the mustard plaster hardened, drawing blood away from the bruise, Rosalie Claire unwrapped it and gently wiped off the sticky gunk. She reached in her pack for a tube of ice-cold gel.

"Arnica. Comes from the prettiest pink flower." She spread it on. It had the fresh scent of summer rain.

"Now your bruise will disappear in half the time."

We were interrupted by Florida's panicky yells. "Where is she?"

Uh-oh. Was I in trouble?

"You'd better skedaddle, Madison. Here—keep the arnica. Apply it every couple of hours. Come back when you can. And don't worry about Leroy. He can stay with me a while. I'll be sure to tie him up before Manny gets home."

Manny? So that was the name of the greasy-haired guy who treated poor Leroy like dirt.

I thanked Rosalie Claire and hurried out the screen door. It banged behind me as I ran into the backyard.

The yelling grew louder. Florida had gone over the edge.

Chapter Twenty

I steeled my nerves and went inside.

My grandmother was in a first-prize panic. "Where is it? Where is it?!"

"It?" Not "she?" That was a relief.

"Where is it? Where's the remote control?" At least she hadn't noticed I'd been gone.

"I have no idea." I shrugged. I was 100 percent sure I'd put it back on the coffee table last night.

"Then I think I know what happened," she hissed. "Your grandfather has hidden it."

Grandpa Jack shuffled from the bedroom in his robe and slippers. "Holy guacamole, can't a guy get a little shut-eye on a Sunday mornin'?"

Florida marched right up to him. "Jack Brown, I want you to tell me where you put my remote control this instant!"

"Right down the ol' garbage disposal where it belongs." Grandpa yawned.

Florida flew to the kitchen, straight for the sink. "How dare you?"

Grandpa snorted out a small chuckle. "I'm jokin', Florida. Relax why don't ya? I'm sure that evil piece of plastic is around here somewhere."

My grandmother was not amused. She squinted her eyes at him, real narrow. "You tell me right now. What did you do with it?"

"Not a blasted thing. We'll find it, though frankly it's the last thing in the world we ought to be doin'. I reckon it would be better if that remote control and your big ol' fancy TV grew legs and made a beeline straight to the county dump."

Florida glared at Grandpa.

Even so, Grandpa joined in and the three of us searched everywhere. We finally gave up. The remote control was definitely missing.

"For the love of Pete, what are you in such a big hurry to buy this mornin'? They got a special on new husbands?" Grandpa chuckled at his own joke, but Florida stared at him steely-eyed.

"For your information, Mister You-Are-Not-Funny, Patsy has been on the hunt for some fabulous accessory to complete the ensemble she's wearing for her anniversary dinner. I thought I'd buy her a little present."

"How charitable," said Grandpa Jack, although he didn't sound as if he meant it.

"Hold on. Never mind—I happen to have just the thing in the garage. I knew that fake fur vest I bought from *The Shopping Mall Network* would come in handy some day."

Uh-oh. We'd sold that fake fur vest at Big Daddy's Flea Market.

Grandpa and I traded horrified looks as Florida raced to the garage, temporarily forgetting about her missing remote control.

"Are we in trouble?" I asked.

"Quite possibly. Guess she was bound to figure it out some year or another."

We sat in the kitchen awaiting the return of Hurricane Florida. All kinds of noises echoed from the garage. Boxes being ripped open, shoved around, and toppled over. There was also a little swearing going on, but I don't want to repeat what I heard. It must have been at least a half-hour before my grandmother came back inside.

"Someone stole my things!" She was spitting mad.

"Well, how about that?" Grandpa used a kitchen knife to pick dirt from under his fingernails.

Wasn't he going to tell her the truth?

"Hand me the phone. I'm calling 911." Florida looked positively fierce.

"Sunshine, can you hand your grandma the telephone?"

I couldn't believe my ears. My grandfather was going to let Florida call the police? He might have been afraid to tell her the truth, but I wasn't. I was sick and tired of all their lies. And now I actually wondered if my grandpa had, after all, hidden the remote control.

"Florida, nobody's been stealing your stuff," I said. "Grandpa and I sold your fur vest and a bunch of your other things at the flea market in Las Cruces. Sorry, Grandpa," I said to him, "but it's the truth."

Grandpa Jack stopped picking at his nails and stared at the floor. There was so much silence the kitchen clock sounded as loud as a ticking time bomb. Then the bomb exploded. With a sonic boom. My grandparents proceeded to have the biggest fight in the history of fights.

Florida screeched at Grandpa.

Grandpa hollered at Florida.

Florida threw silverware and plates. Fortunately, Grandpa ducked in time.

Grandpa smashed a few of Florida's little ceramic poodles on the floor, which might seem funny, but it wasn't at the time.

"Florida, I am sick and tired of all this. Don't expect to see me again until you kick your shopping-show habit for good." And he stomped out of the house.

I ran after him.

"Sorry, Grandpa."

But that was only partly the case. I wasn't sorry for telling the truth. I was just sorry that the truth made them so angry with each other.

Grandpa sighed. "Don't worry about it, Sunshine. I guess I was hopin' for a foolish minute that maybe I'd gotten away with it, so why rock the boat? Better to avoid a scene. Know what I mean?"

"Sort of." I guess if my grandmother thought some burglar had stolen her things, then Grandpa could have kept on doing what he'd been doing for another fourteen years.

"Anyway, I reckon in the long run it's better to have everything out on the table. I suppose you did the right thing, tellin' the truth."

Grandpa kissed me goodbye, got into his truck, slammed the door shut, and drove away.

Florida was in the living room, sweeping up broken bits of shattered plates and poodles. I dug the back-up remote control out of my underwear drawer and gave it to her.

She clutched it to her chest and collapsed on the sofa. "What would I do if I couldn't watch the shopping shows?" she asked. And then she cried. I'd never seen her look that sad. Not even at my mom's funeral.

Chapter Twenty-One

Florida did her best to stay away from the shopping shows.

For the next five days straight, she called in sick at work and watched soap operas, game shows, and reality TV. Whenever she channel-surfed she stopped when she landed on a shopping show. It was as if her remote control button-pushing finger froze on the spot. She'd watch for ten seconds with the saddest look in her eyes, like she was at a party spying on a group of old friends who didn't want to hang out with her anymore. But she didn't buy a single thing. And you know what? I was actually proud of her.

For that first week, packages piled up daily on the doorstep from all the purchases my grandmother had made before going cold turkey. Most likely, those silly hair bows she'd ordered for me were inside one of them. Thankfully, she seemed to have forgotten about them, the way she forgot about so much of the stuff she bought. Before too long, the package deliveries would stop, and the UPS driver would probably think Florida had moved away or died.

Most of the time when Florida was in her TV trance, I taught Leroy tricks. By the end of the week he could sit, stay, roll over, and fetch a ball without popping it. That dog was smart.

I only saw Rosalie Claire once that week. She was outside sweeping her porch four days after Grandpa left.

"I have a confession to make," she said. "When you dropped your sketchbook and ran off into the house with your grandpa the other day, I took a peek. That was a wonderful picture you drew of Leroy. You've got a mighty big talent for such a young girl."

"Thanks," I said.

"Maybe you could sketch a picture of me sometime. That would be nice."

I already had. It was right after I'd arrived, and I'd drawn Rosalie Claire in all her layers, her eyes spinning like pinwheels. It wasn't nice at all. It was goofy and mean.

"Maybe I could," I said as I double-hoped she hadn't flipped the book's pages to see the nasty drawing.

"Where have you been?" I asked her.

"My job at the retirement home. I work with old folks who've lost their memories. Always trying to help them make the here and now a little bit better."

Losing your memory sounded like the saddest thing ever. Sometimes memories are all you have left of a person. And, believe me, I should know.

"I was thinking about baking a blueberry pie. Want to help?"

My mom used to make the best blueberry pie in the history of pies. I hadn't had any since we'd baked one together last summer. I longed for a piece, but I didn't want to chance going over there when Florida was home.

"Thanks, maybe another day," I told her.

"Anytime," she said.

• • •

I kept asking Florida when she was going back to work. "When I'm good and ready," she said as she stared like a zombie at the TV.

I hoped she'd be ready any minute. I wanted to take Rosalie Claire up on her offer of pie. And even more than that, a fluttery feeling in my gut told me she had important secrets I should know.

On Night Number Five of her stay-at-home marathon, Florida finally announced she was returning to work.

"But not before I indulge in a little pampering," she said. "First thing in the morning, Patsy and I are off on a beautification mission. Lucky you—you'll have the day to yourself."

I knew exactly what I was going to do. And I wasn't going to be doing it by myself.

Chapter Twenty-Two

Most of the night I dreamed about making blueberry pie with my mom. I even smelled its sugary sweetness in my dreams, but I awoke to the stench of hairspray. Florida was busy beautifying herself so she could spend the day getting beautified. Go figure. The second she left, I hurried outside and unhooked Leroy.

Then I knocked on Rosalie Claire's back door.

When she answered, an unmistakable fragrance filled the air.

"Good morning, Madison, you're just in time. I just finished baking a pie. Blueberry."

"It's my favorite," I said.

"Mine too."

Leroy followed me inside and sat in his usual spot under the kitchen table.

While Rosalie Claire pulled the pie from the oven and set it on a rack to cool, I studied a framed photograph that hung above the table. In it a man held up a fishing pole with nothing but an empty hook on the end of the line. He was cracking up as if someone had told him a really funny joke.

"That lovely man never could catch a fish to save his life."

"Is that your brother?" I asked.

"No, that's my Thomas. Someday he's going to be my husband."

She told me all about him. They'd met in New Orleans.

"We worked together evenings writing for a neighborhood newspaper called *The Bywater Some Times*. It was named that because we only put out the paper sometimes. Thomas was the kindest man I've ever met. At first, we were just friends."

"And then?"

"And then it turned into something more. The day Hurricane Katrina was on its way, the danger of the situation drove me to tell Thomas the truth. That I loved him. And he confessed he loved me back. When the hurricane hit and we were holed up in the shelter, he proposed."

"But you didn't get married?"

"We decided to wait. My Grandma Daisy was ill, so I came back here to take care of her. Thomas joined me until early last year, and left three months before my grandma died. He bought a restaurant and an old inn down in Costa Rica that he's busy fixing up. It's something he's always wanted to do. Sooner or later I'll join him. But who knows when? That lovely man can be slower than molasses in January when he takes on a project."

I hoped he'd be super-slow. I didn't want Rosalie Claire leaving anytime soon. I was just getting to know her.

"I have an idea. How about we pack up this pie and take a stroll over to the park? We can have a picnic and do a little catch-and-release fishing."

"Sounds perfect," I said.

While Rosalie Claire carefully wrapped the pie in foil and slipped it into a straw picnic basket, I tied Leroy back up in his yard.

By the time I returned she had two fishing poles she'd retrieved from the garage. Then she pulled a windbreaker over her sweater, even though the morning was hot and still.

We headed toward downtown T or C—that's what the locals called Truth or Consequences. I crossed my fingers, hoping and praying we wouldn't run into Florida.

We passed house after house, their yards dotted with rocks, tumbleweeds, and not much more. We didn't spy a single person, dog, cat, or living or breathing thing. Nothing. The only amazing part was the sky with white fluffy clouds drifting overhead.

"My favorite thing to do here is to watch those clouds," Rosalie Claire said.

"Mine too," I told her. What else was there to do in this town? "Did you grow up here?"

"I moved here to live with my Grandma Daisy the summer I turned fifteen. She was my rock after my folks passed."

"They died? Both of them? How?"

"A car accident. In the days before seatbelts."

"I'm sorry," I said.

Wow. I'd just asked her the same question I hated everyone asking me. Maybe next time when someone asked how my mom died, I'd cut them a little slack.

"That was the hardest time of my life," she said. "But Grandma Daisy stood by me. I lived with her until I left for college."

The same as Florida and me. Only Florida wasn't exactly my rock. More like a thorn in my side.

"When she died Grandma Daisy left me the house. Guess I'll have to sell it when I move to Costa Rica. I think you would have liked her," she said. "She was the first African American woman to move here back in the 1960s. Opened up a little shop that sold crystals and herbs. Healing stuff. Grandma loved this little town. She always said it had magic in the air."

We crossed onto Main Street and Rosalie Claire pointed up ahead to an old adobe storefront.

"That's my grandma's old shop. Wildflower Mercantile. Still in business. Years ago they carried fanny packs just like mine. Even today it's the only place for miles around that still sells magic potions and healing stones."

As we passed by we peered into its dusty windows filled with crystal balls, jars of herbs, and dancing rays of rainbow light.

When I looked up, I felt a stab of fear in my stomach. Florida and Patsy were halfway up the block, heading our way. I wished I could disappear into a crack in the sidewalk. What was I going to do? I noticed the Visitors' Center, right next door.

"Let's check this place out!" I ducked inside and Rosalie Claire followed me.

I pretended to study a bulletin board that stood on wheels in the middle of the room. It was covered with modern-day photos of Truth or Consequences. All the while I kept on the lookout for Florida. I reminded myself that she was on a beautification mission so this would probably be the last place she'd come.

When I could hear Florida and Patsy's chatter echoing from the sidewalk, I darted behind the bulletin board. My heart pounded like a jackhammer.

Something caught my eye while I waited. On the flip side of the bulletin board were old black-and-white photos of the town. Truth or Consequences looked almost exactly the same, but underneath the pictures it said: HOT SPRINGS. Weird.

Thankfully, the giddy voices faded down the street. The coast was clear.

"Why does it say the town has a different name?" I asked Rosalie Claire.

"It's the funniest story. Back in 1950, the local folks voted to change it on account of a contest. At the time, *Truth or Consequences* was a popular radio show. The host, Ralph Edwards, said the first town to officially change its name to match the show would win. Said he'd personally show up to broadcast his program once a year. This town was the only one to take him up on his offer."

Wow. That seemed kind of lame to me.

"The people in town thought it would get them a lot of publicity and bring in a flood of tourists," Rosalie Claire explained.

Judging by the empty streets, I guessed it hadn't worked out so well.

"Now, are you ready to try your hand at a little fishing?" she asked.

I nodded and we headed for the door. Above it I noticed a long banner with big bold letters. It said: HELLO THERE! WE'VE BEEN WAITING FOR YOU!

"That's what Ralph Edwards said at the beginning of every show," Rosalie Claire said. "It's the town's unofficial slogan."

I got that same fluttery feeling in my stomach. Had Truth or Consequences been waiting for me? It was just a stupid old slogan—right?

Or was it?

Chapter Twenty-Three

Ralph Edwards Park was at the far end of town. When we got to the pond, we sat in the shadiest spot under a cottonwood tree.

Rosalie Claire shivered.

How could anybody be cold in this weather? By now I realized I could probably ask her anything. So I did.

"I've always got a chill," she told me. "You know what they say: cold hands, warm heart. Well, I figure I must be warm down to my soul since I'm always freezing."

So that's why she wore so many layers of clothes.

"My mom would have taken me to the doctor if I was putting on that many sweaters."

"I suppose she would have," she said. "Duly noted."

Then Rosalie Claire unzipped her fanny pack.

"Let me see. . . ." She rummaged around and pulled out two hooks with yellow feathers attached and a big jar of wriggling worms. As always, her pack contained just what was needed.

"I'm not too good at this," I told her. "I only caught two things when I went fishing with my best friend Violet on Bainbridge Island—a plastic vegetable bag and an old sneaker."

Rosalie Claire laughed. "It just takes patience. And the right-colored fly. Yellow feathers for sunny weather and red feathers when it's cloudy."

She showed me how to thread the worm on my hook, and then she helped me cast my fishing line way out into the middle of the shimmering pond.

We hadn't been fishing for more than two minutes when something tugged my line.

"Well, it appears that you have much better fishing luck than my Thomas."

Rosalie Claire helped me reel in a twelve-inch trout, which was way more exciting than catching a plastic bag or an old shoe.

The fish flopped like mad as I carefully worked it off the hook. I was trying not to hurt it since we planned on throwing it back. I poked my finger on the sharp tip of the hook.

Blood spurted out. "Ouch!"

Rosalie Claire had me press on the puncture to seal the wound. She released the fish back into the water, unzipped her fanny pack, and pulled out a Band-Aid and a tube of Neosporin.

"It's like you have everything in the world in there."

"Not everything. Just the things I need." She spread ointment on the inside of the bandage and wrapped it tight around my finger.

"But how do you know what to bring? Or is it . . . magic?"

"You tell me. My Grandma Daisy gave me this fanny pack for my eighteenth birthday. I've collected all sorts of things and stuffed them in there. Whenever I look inside, there are things I've put in and things that have just shown up. Every time I have to help somebody out, I find just what I need."

"Sounds like magic to me," I told her.

"Me too," she agreed.

"Between your pouch and the MegaPix, I think your grandma was right about there being magic in the air."

"You know, every single day I wish she was still around so I could ask her more about it. She knew more about magic than I ever will."

I knew exactly what she meant. At least 100 times a day, I wished my mom was around so I could ask her stuff.

We cast our lines again. If only I could tell my mom about the fanny pack, the MegaPix, and the magic. She'd always changed the subject whenever I talked about magic, probably because she didn't believe in it. I wished I could tell her it was real.

Just then I felt another bite.

"You've got the gift, girl!"

I reeled in another trout. This time Rosalie Claire guided it off the hook and let me throw it back. Then she got so quiet I could hear the fish swishing away in the water.

"In fact, you have the gift just like your mama."

I couldn't believe my ears. "You knew my mom?"

"I wanted to tell you the first day I met you, but the time had to be right. I guess your grandma didn't mention she and I went to Hot Springs High together?"

"Uh-uh." I tried to picture Florida and Rosalie Claire as teenagers together at school. Weird.

"Your mama was born not long after I left for college. Once she was about seven she started spending a lot of time with my grandma. Whenever I'd come to town to visit, Angela would run over and we'd spend the most precious times together. I used to bring her to this very spot to fish. We'd talk and talk."

"My mom always had a lot to say."

Rosalie Claire's eyes crinkled with the memory. "She sure did. When she was about your age, she told me the funniest story. Your grandma used to make her wear nothing but fussy little dresses. Well, your mama couldn't stand it. By the time she was eight, she'd figured out those little dresses were worth something. Every time she was forced to wear some fancy get-up, she'd run straight down to Thrifty Treasures on Main Street and trade in her dress for a pair of used jeans and an old T-shirt."

I thought of the pink cupcake dress Florida had tried to buy me. It made me happy to know just how much my mom and I were alike.

"Finally, your grandma gave up. When your mama had something she wanted to do, her will was mightier than a southern New Mexico sandstorm. She had spunk. And big dreams.

"I remember once when I came through T or C after a trip I'd made to Russia. Your mama must have been about fourteen or fifteen. I was wearing a necklace I'd bought in Moscow—a little red Firebird charm on a chain. Legend has it Firebirds live 500 years, then burst into flame and give birth to another Firebird. Well, your mama was fixated on that necklace. She couldn't take her eyes off it. I think it was because she so badly wanted to be as free as a bird to start living the life *she* wanted to live. Not the one your Grandma Florida had planned for her."

"Do you still have the necklace?" I really wanted to see something my mom had loved so much when she was a kid.

"No. I gave it to her. She needed it more than I did. She wore that necklace for years."

That must be what she was wearing in the photo Grandpa had shown me.

"You know, Madison, I remember the day you were born," Rosalie Claire said. "Your mama called me the very next morning. It was the happiest day of her life."

That's how she knew my name.

"I sure do miss her," I said quietly.

"Yeah, I miss her too."

Before you knew it, we were both wiping away tears.

"Looks like we could both use some cheering up. Ready for a nice slice of pie?" Rosalie Claire asked.

I nodded, so she lifted the pie from the basket and peeled back the warm layer of tinfoil. She cut two fat slices and slid them onto paper plates.

"Mmm-mm. It tastes just like my mom's." I savored the first bite and pretended she was the one who'd really made it.

"I'm not surprised, since we both learned from the pie master herself—Grandma Daisy."

"Did Florida mind that my mom spent so much time with you and your grandma?"

"At first it made her furious, but eventually she just gave in. There was no controlling Angela once she set her mind to something. I think your grandma was unhappy it was always Grandma Daisy or me your mama ran to when she needed to talk things through."

Then Rosalie Claire looked at me, all serious.

"When you went into the Visitors' Center back there, it was because you didn't want Florida to catch you with 'the crazy lady.' Am I right?"

"You're not crazy," I told her.

"Now you know that. At first you didn't."

"Yeah, I guess so," I said. "She doesn't want me hanging out with you."

"It would probably be best to tell her anyway, Madison. Carrying around secrets can make your head hurt and your heart ache. Truth is usually best."

She was right. I decided that it was time to tell Florida all about Rosalie Claire.

Chapter Twenty-Four

Florida's car wasn't in the driveway when we returned to Grape Street, and I breathed a sigh of relief.

Rosalie Claire wrapped her arms around me in a big warm hug. "That's the best day I've had in a long time."

"Me too. See you soon?"

"Of course," she said. "And best of luck with your grandma."

"Thanks, I'll need it."

Back in the house I waited on the sofa for Florida and tried to pass the time sketching pictures in my book. But I couldn't concentrate. What would happen when I told Florida the truth about Rosalie Claire? Would she kick me out? Lock me in my room? I started to get cold feet.

I noticed the remote control sitting on the coffee table. I couldn't take my eyes off of it, as if some mysterious force pulled at me. Was I possessed? Even though Rosalie Claire had warned me about the possible dangers of deep magic, I longed to escape—and it seemed safer than facing Florida. But where should I go?

I flipped through the channels, trying to decide. A reality TV show about fashion models? No way. Another shopping show? No thanks. A news report from Paris? Hmm. I wondered if that would transport me closer to Violet. Could I zap into the city of Paris and find her waiting for me?

I pushed the purple button and the ENTER button at the same time. The words popped up on the screen.

As I was about to push again, Florida walked through the door. Her hair looked like it had burst into flame. It was as orangey red as a desert sunset. I quickly switched off the TV and tossed the remote control onto the table. No escaping now.

"Well, honey, tell me what you think! Isn't it utterly divine?" She twirled in prima ballerina circles.

"Wow, it's so *red*. And yeah, it's, uh, really divine." I'm pretty sure that was the first time in my entire life I'd used the word divine, but I could tell it made her happy.

Then she asked The Question.

"So, Darling, what fabulous thing did you do today? Tell Florida *everything*."

Wow, she'd never wanted to hear anything about me before. All I could figure was that she was in a really good mood because of her new hairdo. It was time to tell the truth.

My knees began to wobble and I considered chickening out. But I knew I couldn't keep my secret forever. I inhaled a little courage.

"I spent the day with Rosalie Claire."

Florida's happiness faded fast. Her eyebrows scrunched up, and she looked like a fierce bull ready to charge.

"Excuse me? What part of 'she's crazy' was not crystal clear, young lady?"

"She's not crazy, Florida. Not at all."

"How dare you contradict me! When I say that woman is crazy, she is crazy, do you understand me?" Her breath came fast and her face was tight.

Then I just said what I thought. Actually I yelled it. I probably shouldn't have, but I really and truly had to say what was on my mind. "You don't like Rosalie Claire because my mom liked her and her Grandma Daisy better than she liked you!"

Florida glared at me with fiery eyes. Then she screeched at the top of her lungs. "Madison McGee, I forbid you to spend time with that woman again. Now sit your fanny down where I can keep an eye on you. I am heating up two TV dinners, and tonight we are watching TV."

Ugh. I'd have preferred it if she'd sent me to my room, rather than being sentenced to sit next to her watching her channel-surf through her dumb TV shows.

But tomorrow Florida wouldn't be able to keep an eye on me at all. She was going back to work.

Chapter Twenty-Five

The second my grandmother left the next morning, I raced over to Rosalie Claire's. On her back door was a note.

Good Morning, Madison!
Sorry but I'm working double-shifts the next few days. Come in and help yourself to pie. xoxo
                                        Rosalie Claire

I went inside, found the pie in the refrigerator and cut myself a wedge. From the first taste to the last, it made me miss my mom.

Back at Florida's I considered going into the TV again, but only because I wanted to escape my boredom. There was another rerun of *Just Jessica*. Could I zap back and at least hang out with Allison? But the second Carlee Knight popped on screen the whole nightmare flooded back, and I switched off the TV.

And I had Leroy to keep me company. That week we were close to perfecting what I thought would be the best trick in all of dog history.

On the fifth day when I went into the yard to unhook him, Rosalie Claire was hanging up her laundry. There wasn't a single sweater or sweatshirt clipped to the line. Just cool summer tops and cotton capris.

"Good morning, Madison! Sure is a nice warm morning!"

"You're not wearing layers." For the first time ever, Rosalie Claire had on a short-sleeved summer dress.

"Nope. A little blue pill a day fixed my thyroid problem and heated me up as fast as a furnace in Indian summer. Sure is nice to feel warmed by the sun. And thank you, by the way."

"For what?"

"For talking me into making a doctor's appointment."

"You're welcome. I'm happy you're feeling better."

Leroy trotted over to Rosalie Claire and licked her bare brown legs. She scratched him on his favorite spot behind his ear, then treated him to beef jerky from her fanny pack.

Then Leroy and I demonstrated The Trick. I sang "Queen of My Doublewide Trailer" while Leroy stood on his hind legs and danced, grinning ear-to-ear.

• • •

Two weeks after Florida went cold turkey off her shopping shows was the day that everything changed. She was working at the flower shop, and I was alone. I headed outside to draw. I thought Rosalie Claire would be at work too, but she wasn't. I hadn't been out there for more than ten minutes when she came outside and began to sweep clouds of dust off her back porch.

"Good morning, Madison. What masterpiece are you creating today?" she asked.

"Leroy wearing a French beret." I showed her my sketch.

"Promise me you'll keep drawing all your life. You're very talented."

"Promise," I said.

As I headed back to the porch to set down my drawing supplies, a strange hiss filled the air reminding me of sprinklers going off, but the day was as dry as anything.

Leroy whimpered.

I turned toward the noise. A long brown snake with dark diamond markings slithered toward my bare feet, shaking its rattley tail.

"Rattlesnake," Rosalie Claire hissed. "Don't move."

A one-bite-and-I'd-be-dead-meat rattlesnake? I froze solid as the snake edged closer.

Rosalie Claire grabbed a shovel, hoisted it above her head and lunged. I shut my eyes tight, not wanting to see.

THWACK!

Then all I heard were Leroy's whimpers, my thundering heartbeat, and a hummingbird zipping by with a whirr.

"You can look," she said.

The rattlesnake lay dead in the dirt, just inches in front of my feet, its head cut clean off. And if that rattlesnake wasn't at least four feet long, my name isn't Madison McGee.

How do you thank someone who just saved your life? I leaped into her arms and hugged her tight.

"What would I do without you, Rosalie Claire?" Tears ran down my cheeks. I looked up and they were running down hers too.

"I think we deserve some nice cold lemonade," she said. "I'll give that scoundrel a proper burial later."

We climbed her back steps and went inside.

Together we squeezed a pitcher full of real lemon juice and mixed it up with cups and cups of sugar. The kitchen was filled with the sound of squishing lemons and the clinkety-clank of the big metal spoon against the glass pitcher. She poured two glasses and cut us each a piece of blueberry pie.

"You know, my Grandma Daisy won the pie contest every single year at the Sierra County Fair."

"I always told my mom she should enter her pie at our county fair, but she never did."

"Perhaps *you're* meant to do that. If you learn to make it as good as your mama did, then someday you can win the blue ribbon," Rosalie Claire said.

"Maybe. Although maybe I don't have to learn since you always seem to have some around," I joked.

Rosalie Claire folded her hands together, her forehead knotted up, and she stared into space.

"Madison, I have something to tell you. I heard from Thomas yesterday." Her eyes filled with tears.

"Is he okay?"

"He's more than okay. He is as lovely and funny and amazing as ever."

"Why are you so sad?"

"Everything's ready. He's finished the inn. I fly to Costa Rica the day after tomorrow."

"For a vacation?" I asked.

"Forever. We're getting married."

Then it hit me. Rosalie Claire was leaving me. I would be doomed to live the rest of my life alone with my lousy, self-centered grandmother in Truth or Consequences, New Mexico.

"I'm coming with you."

Rosalie Claire leaned in close and wrapped her hands around mine. "There is nothing in the world I would love more than to have you come down to Costa Rica and live with Thomas and me. But your grandmother . . ." Her voice trailed into silence.

A hard lump grew in my throat. "I don't care what she thinks. She doesn't even want me! Maybe she'd let me go with you. My mom would want me to go with you."

Then I couldn't help myself. I cried as hard as I had the night my mother died.

Rosalie Claire cradled me in her arms and rocked me back and forth for what seemed like hours. She held me until there were no tears left.

"Talk to your grandma. But it would be best not to get your hopes up. And if you can't come, please know I will never lose touch. I'll visit when I can."

Visiting wasn't good enough. I was determined to leave on that airplane with Rosalie Claire.

Chapter Twenty-Six

I hatched my plan. Operation Madison McBratt.

I'd be so obnoxious that Florida would *beg* me to leave. I'd pretend to be as horrible as Carlee Knight and Molly Cooper combined. Or even more horrible. I got to work immediately.

I left candy wrappers on the floor and told Florida to clean them up.

I refused to throw away my TV dinner tray.

I swiped the remote control right out of Florida's hand and switched the show to a nature channel.

Florida became more and more furious with me. That night, when I brought Leroy into the house right under her nose, she told me it was the last straw. She sent me to my room.

I refused to go.

Oh boy, did she yell. "You ungrateful, good-for-nothing horrid little girl," she screamed. "After all I've done for you! I've fed you and clothed you and taken you in when no one else wanted you. How dare you treat me this way?!"

Operation Madison McBratt seemed to be working. It was time to act.

"Well, now there is someone else who wants me and I'm leaving!"

I sprinted to my bedroom and yanked my suitcase out from under the bed. As fast as I could, I crammed in my clothes and my mom's ferry jacket.

"Where do you think you're going, young lady?" Florida was at my door, her hands planted firmly on her hips.

"Costa Rica. Rosalie Claire is moving there, and I'm going with her."

Florida's hands clenched into tight balls. She looked like she wanted to punch me.

"I don't know what shenanigans that woman is up to," she snarled, "or what spell she's cast over you, but there is no way on God's green earth that you are going anywhere with her. Nowhere! Do you understand?"

"You can't stop me," I yelled. But in truth I knew she could.

Florida knew she could too. She grounded me for a week. She made me go to my room and she even locked my bedroom window. When I begged her to at least let me say goodbye to Rosalie Claire, she refused.

"Thank goodness the old witch is leaving," she spat.

I curled up on my bed with my mom's old ferry jacket and hid beneath its thick fabric. I could barely make out the scent of cinnamon and butterscotch. It seemed to be fading away.

My head spun with a million sad thoughts. I've always tried my best not to feel sorry for myself, but not on that night. It didn't seem fair that my mom died. Or that I didn't even have a dad to move in with. Just my crazy grandmother, Florida Brown. My mom used to say it's a fact that sometimes life isn't fair. I didn't know what she meant until she was gone.

When I slipped into the hallway to go to the bathroom, Florida jumped up from her TV watching to make sure I wasn't trying to escape. That night I fell asleep to the sound of Leroy howling in the backyard.

The next morning I figured maybe Florida would have cooled off. Boy, was I wrong. She was still super-mean and made me stay in my room. I kept trying to figure out how I might escape my pink bedroom jail, but Florida was my prison guard. I was sure if I tried to sneak out my window, she'd catch me and ground me until it was time to go to college.

Rosalie Claire would be leaving for good tomorrow, and it was haunting me. I wished I had a hammer so I could break all the clocks to make time stand still.

Mostly I sketched pictures of Rosalie Claire and me, so I could always remember us together.

I kept looking out my window hoping to catch a glimpse of her. Twice she came into the yard, squinting over at our house, as if she was searching for me. Then she'd sigh and head back inside, letting her creaky screen door slam shut.

After dinner that night, all the lights switched off at her house. A few minutes later our doorbell rang. I could hear the voices of my grandmother and Rosalie Claire. The conversation sounded friendly enough, and then Florida cracked open my door.

She wasn't friendly with me. Not at all. She was tense, and she hissed through her teeth: "Go say goodbye to your precious Rosalie Claire, and make it fast. The airport shuttle is picking her up in ten minutes. I'll be watching television—and I'll also be watching the clock."

Ten minutes? I'd thought she wasn't leaving until the next day! I raced past Florida and flew out the front door, right into Rosalie Claire's open arms.

"My flight leaves early in the morning, so I'm staying at the Super-8 by the airport tonight. Let's go someplace and talk."

We walked over to Rosalie Claire's front yard and sat on her garden bench. I hoped and prayed she had come up with a plan to take me along.

"I wish more than anything you could come with me, but right now you need to stay with your grandma. Although winds can always change, Madison."

I didn't feel a single bit of wind. Not even the tiniest breeze. All I felt was the hot choking air of Truth or Consequences.

"Why doesn't Thomas move here and open his inn and a restaurant? Why does it have to be in Costa Rica?"

"It was our dream to do this together and to live by the sea. It's my destiny," she said quietly.

"But what about my destiny?"

"I have a very good feeling about your destiny, Madison McGee. And you must know that we will always be together. You are like a golden thread that will be connected to my heart no matter where we are."

The airport shuttle pulled into the driveway. Time was slipping away.

"I have something for you. I was looking through my pouch this morning and this showed up." She unzipped her fanny pack and pulled out a bright-red bird charm dangling on a silver chain. At first I thought it was the necklace my mom had worn in the photograph, although I knew that wasn't possible.

"It's a Firebird. The same kind I gave to your mama when she was not much older than you. I guess the pouch meant for you to have one too."

She cupped it into my hand. "Now whenever you wear this it will remind you of your mama and our summer together."

"I'll wear it every single day, just like my mom."

Rosalie Claire fastened it around my neck. I tucked it inside my T-shirt so it could stay close to my heart. We hugged each other tight until we were interrupted by the shuttle driver's honk.

"Guess he's in a hurry," she said.

Then it occurred to me. I had something for Rosalie Claire. "Please don't leave. I'll be right back!"

I sped into Florida's house and carefully tore one of the pictures I'd drawn of the two of us from my sketchbook. By the time I raced back outside, the driver had loaded Rosalie Claire's suitcases into the Super Shuttle van.

"For you," I said.

She took the drawing and tears filled her brown sugar eyes. "This is the greatest gift you could have given me, Madison. See? It's proof we will always be together."

We hugged and then she took my face in her hands.

"And promise me—no more going into the TV, okay?"

"I promise."

After one final hug she was gone.

I stood on the sidewalk watching until the van's tail lights disappeared from sight. It was then that I noticed the FOR SALE sign that had been hammered into a gravel bed in front of Rosalie Claire's darkened house.

The orange glow of the TV flickered through Florida's front window. I couldn't face her just yet. The certainty of spending the next seven years of my life living with her tied my stomach into knots.

Even though my ten minutes was up, I went into the backyard to cuddle with Leroy. Through the sliding glass doors, I could see Florida flipping through the TV channels.

Tears streamed down my cheeks and Leroy licked them up as fast as they fell. Then he wriggled to his feet, dragging his heavy chain behind the computer monitor. He began to dig. To my amazement, he unearthed my old dead soccer ball. He picked it up with his teeth, all dirty and tattered, then trotted over and dropped it at my feet. I think it was Leroy's way of trying to make me feel better.

I sat outside that night, stroking his soft fur until the full moon rose over Rosalie Claire's old house. I was kind of surprised Florida hadn't come looking for me.

When I finally went inside, she wasn't there. At the time I thought maybe she'd gone to the bathroom. But the bathroom door was open and the light was off. She wasn't in her bedroom, or mine, or the kitchen. Her gold Cadillac was still parked in the driveway.

Back in the living room I noticed the remote control on the floor. Then I had that feeling again—the slight fluttering sensation in my belly. I looked at the TV and there was my grandmother.

She'd been zapped into the reality TV show *Stranded in the Amazon!*

Chapter Twenty-Seven

My first thought? Leave Florida in the TV and figure out a way to get myself to the airport so I could fly to Costa Rica.

But that thought lasted only a second. Florida was on television, lined up in the Amazon jungle with a group of contestants, on the verge of throwing a major hissy fit.

Even though I'd just promised Rosalie Claire I would stay out of the TV, I knew what I had to do.

I picked up the remote control and pushed the two buttons. Ping! Was I sure I wanted to choose that channel? I didn't have a choice, did I? I had to save my grandmother!

In a flash I was transported somewhere in the Amazon rainforest. A sweaty camera guy was videotaping the contestants. It was early morning, and the air was already sticky and hot. I was met by a concert of wild noises. Birds twittered, bugs buzzed, and monkeys chattered.

But the loudest noise in the rainforest? My grandmother.

"Excuse me! Would somebody please tell me what is going on here?" She was so mad I could picture cartoon steam pouring from her ears.

I stuffed the remote into the waistband of my shorts and scurried over to take my place beside her.

"Sorry I'm late," I apologized to the perfectly tanned TV host. Florida gave me the oddest look, and who could blame her? I mean, if you'd never zapped into a TV show before and didn't know how it all worked, it would be awfully confusing.

"Madison McGee, we've been waiting for you! Let the competition begin!"

He lifted a brass trumpet, playing that song you always hear at the beginning of horse races.

"What in the devil is going on?" Florida sputtered as the trumpet blared.

"It's the MegaPix TV," I whispered. "It's magic."

"Oh, for heaven sake, do you really expect me to believe something that ridiculous? Tell me the truth, young lady!" The trumpet had stopped.

"Cut!" yelled the director. He was big as a blimp and covered from head to toe in an outfit made completely out of mosquito netting.

"Do we have a problem, people?" He peered at Florida through white mesh.

"Yes we do, Mister Whoever-You-Are. My granddaughter and I need to go have a little chat."

At least she called me her granddaughter.

"Make it quick. We've got a show to shoot here, Mrs. Brown."

Florida marched straight for the riverbank. I trotted after her until we were out of sight and out of earshot. Only a fuzzy-faced white-bellied spider monkey perched on a tree was listening.

"Explain this instant, and no nonsense." She looked fierce.

"It really and truly is the MegaPix," I said. "Remember when Mike the delivery guy said it would put you in the action like no other TV? He wasn't kidding."

I slid the remote control out of the top of my shorts.

"It's magic. I used this to zap into *Just Jessica* and Alan Stone's shopping show. He made me demonstrate vacuum cleaners. He's not very nice."

"Do you really expect me to believe that? You're making this up."

"I'm telling the truth. How else do you explain that one minute you were in your living room pushing a couple of buttons on the remote when your vision got blurry and your body tingled—and the next minute you wound up on this TV show?"

"How did you know that my body . . . ?" Her voice trailed off and her eyes opened wide with horror. "Oh my goodness, you're right! Well don't just stand there. Get us out of here, pronto!"

"I've never tried it with two people before. Hope it works."

I positioned my fingers over the two buttons.

"Well if that isn't the wackiest thing to bring to the Amazon! Hate to break it to you, sweetheart, but you're not going to be watching a lot of television in the rainforest."

My stomach knotted up.

It was the TV host.

"I'll take that. You know the rules. Bring along only the things we give you."

He snatched the remote right out of my hand.

"You have no right to do that!" Florida planted her hands on her hips.

"Of course I do, Mrs. Brown, because this is my show and I make the rules. She can have it back when you've finished the competition." He shoved it into an oversized pocket in his perfectly ironed safari jacket.

The spider monkey cackled as if this was all some big joke.

With a plastered-on TV-star mega-smile, the host stuck out his hand. "We haven't properly met. I'm Wolf Adams."

"Madison McGee," I said. I knew who he was. He'd been on TV ever since I was little. Wolf Adams had hosted *Stranded on Bora-Bora, Stranded in the Gobi Desert, Stranded in the Outback,* and *Stranded in Any Other Out-in-the-Middle-of-Nowhere-Place-You-Can-Imagine.* I'm surprised he hadn't done a show called *Stranded on Uranus.* In each show a parent and their kid teamed up to compete against other teams of parents and kids to win a million dollars.

Besides, who could forget a man who resembled a giant, inflatable Ken doll?

Sometimes I'd watched the shows with Violet. She loved them. She always got mad at the contestants who were mean to each other. On one episode a boy put a bunch of baby snakes in a girl's sleeping bag to get back at her after she accidentally-on-purpose dumped out his drinking water. That's how nasty these shows could get.

Florida was not going to like this one bit.

"Are you ready to do this?" he asked.

Did it really matter? By now I had enough experience with this zapping business to know it was going to happen whether we wanted it to or not.

"This way, ladies. Follow me." Wolf Adams set out to rejoin the group.

Florida didn't budge. "I am not going to be part of this foolishness, and he can't make me."

"Good luck. It doesn't really work that way," I said.

"Oh, it won't take luck, honey—just a little finesse and the skilled application of my womanly ways. Watch and learn."

She sashayed over to Wolf Adams.

"Excuse me, Mr. Adams," she said super-sweetly, tapping him on his back.

He spun around.

"I mean, Wolf. I can call you Wolf, can't I?"

He nodded as she gazed up at him with twinkly eyes and a movie star smile that sparkled even bigger and brighter than his. My grandmother was actually flirting with Wolf Adams!

"You had a question, Mrs. Brown?"

"You *must* call me Florida. Wolf, you are positively the most divine man I have ever met. And as much as I'd simply adore spending time with you and your friends, I believe there's been the teensiest mistake. You see, Madison and I aren't actually supposed to be here. It was all some kind of silly accident."

She batted her eyelashes at him, which probably didn't make the impression she was hoping for. The air was so hot and moist that her mascara had melted, encircling her eyes like a raccoon.

"It can't possibly be an accident. You're here because we picked you. Because we think you're special."

"Well, of course I'm special. And thank you for noticing. But there was a little mix-up with our fancy new TV and—"

"There's never been a mix-up," he interrupted. "We select our contestants very carefully. Besides, I'd say a fine-looking spitfire like you has a good chance of winning the million dollars, if you play your cards right."

"A million dollars?" Florida's eyes grew wide and her grin grew even wider. "Why, I do declare you're right. There's been no mix-up at all. Let's get this show on the road. I do believe this might be my lucky day!"

Chapter Twenty-Eight

As you can see, it didn't take much for Florida to decide that being on *Stranded in the Amazon* was the best thing that had ever happened to her. All it took was the possibility of winning a million dollars.

Okay, I admit that's a whole bunch of money, but she'd never watched a Wolf Adams show before. She had no idea what she was getting herself into. I knew, and I wanted to skedaddle us out of there before things got nasty.

I needed to retrieve that remote control—and fast.

The cameras rolled the second we rejoined the contestants, so I didn't have a chance to come up with a plan. Trying to pickpocket Wolf Adams right on television wasn't the best idea. I'd have to wait until the time was right.

Florida put on her most dazzling smile while Wolf Adams introduced the show and the contestants. I think she finally realized she was actually on television. She probably wanted to look as much like a movie star as possible.

The odd thing was I was somewhere in South America and probably not far from Costa Rica, geographically speaking. But I was pretty sure that being stuck in MegaPix TV time didn't let me leave the regular way. Not by bus, not by train, not on foot. Just by remote control. Which Wolf Adams had stashed deep in the pocket of his jungle jacket.

During the introduction, I learned a lot of cool facts about the

Amazon rainforest. At least some of it was cool. Some of it made me wish I was boarding that plane to Costa Rica.

The cool stuff? The Amazon rainforest is more than a *billion* acres. There are so many trees and other things growing here that they produce almost 20 percent of the oxygen for the whole entire earth. That's why they call it the "lungs of the planet." It rains *nine* feet a year. And nearly half of all the animal species in the world live here.

The part that wasn't cool? Bugs, bugs, and more bugs. There are *thirty million* kinds of bugs living in the jungle. And at that moment it felt as if at least a million of them had decided that my arms and legs made a tasty breakfast.

"Let's introduce our contestants!" Wolf Adams walked along our line-up as he talked directly into the camera. "We have four teams consisting of one parent and one child, or in one case, a grandmother and grand-daughter. They are about to begin the adventure of a lifetime. For fifteen days they will be stranded in a world filled with wonder and danger."

"Fifteen days?" Florida gasped.

"Each team will have to work together to survive in this wild trop-ical rainforest," he continued. "In the end, it will be the audience at home who will vote and decide which team best excelled at their tasks. And that team will be the one to walk away with the million-dollar prize! Which team will it be?"

"It had better be us," Florida whispered to me.

"I hope not," I whispered back. I really didn't want to be stranded in the Amazon with my grandmother for fifteen whole days. I wanted to get my hands on that remote control and zap us out of there lickety-split.

As the camera followed, Wolf Adams introduced the contestants. Rob and his daughter, Jenna. Carmen and her son, Victor. Kevin and his son, Noah. And then Florida and me. I'm sure I was the only person who was NOT excited to be there.

Each team was given a pair of matching bandanas. Rob and Jenna got pink. Carmen and Victor got blue. Kevin and Noah got green. Florida and I got red. Florida was sure that getting her favorite color was a sign she was going to win the money. She was so happy that she jumped up and kissed Wolf Adams smack on the cheek, leaving behind a bright smudge of red lipstick. Right on national television. I was so embarrassed!

After everyone tied their bandanas around their necks, we all hiked down to the riverbank. There were four painted metal canoes waiting— one red, one blue, one pink, one green. Wolf Adams called them our "primitive vessels." Primitive was right. The boats were made from old pounded-out oil drums.

He handed each team a backpack for our essentials. As we completed each challenge we would earn more things to add to our packs. Florida unzipped ours, peered inside, and let out a shriek.

"What, no makeup? No shampoo? Not even a hairbrush? Do these people not understand the meaning of the word 'essential'? I do hope they have some decent beauty products wherever we're staying tonight."

If wearing bugs all over your body was considered a decent beauty product, she wouldn't have a thing to worry about.

Here's what we did have: one can of bug spray, a bottle of sunscreen, two sets of rain gear, two canteens filled with fresh water, plus the map we needed to help us find our base camp. And they also gave each grown-up a heavy machete to whack our way through the thick, over-grown rainforest.

Florida handed me the machete. "You carry this. I wouldn't begin to know how to use it."

Somehow I wound up with the backpack too. I slathered on the sunscreen so I wouldn't burn and covered myself in bug spray so those thirty million bugs would quit bugging me. When I was done, I passed them to Florida. She complained about the smell of the bug spray because it hid the scent of her Jungle Gardenia perfume. But she put it on anyway.

While Florida was busy rubbing in sunscreen, Jenna, the other girl contestant, wandered over. I wasn't surprised. She'd been staring at me since I'd arrived, which I thought was kind of freaky. She looked over her shoulder, probably to make sure the cameras weren't recording our conversation. They weren't.

"You totally look like that girl on *Just Jessica*," she said. "The one who played Ashley's obnoxious cousin?"

Florida opened her mouth to say something, but thankfully she became distracted by a swarm of bugs that got stuck in the lotion on her legs.

"I do? Thanks." I really didn't want to explain MegaPix magic to a total stranger. She'd probably think I was nuts.

"I didn't see that episode," I said. Which was true because I'd been busy being *on* the episode. All I'd really seen were the credits.

"I auditioned for that show once. They would have cast me, but they said I was too beautiful." She shook her perfect wavy blond hair as if she were in one of those shampoo commercials. Probably just the kind of hair Florida wished I had.

"That's too bad," I said.

"Yeah, it sucked. Actually, I think they're waiting to cast me in a better role. Anyway, being on *Stranded* will definitely give me exposure. It's my golden ticket to my own TV show. Just think—you can say you knew me when."

Wow, I didn't even know her now.

"But it was totally awesome meeting Carlee Knight," she told me. "After my audition, I hung out with her on the set the rest of the day. She is the coolest, nicest person ever."

"She seems nice on TV." But knowing the real Carlee Knight, I highly doubted Jenna's story. "Did she give you her autograph?"

"She did. And she wanted mine because she was sure I'd be famous someday."

Right then I knew she was lying.

"Bet you're jealous," she added.

"Not really."

She looked disappointed.

Jenna kicked at the ground with the toe of her sneaker. Then she looked me square in the eye. "By the way, my dad and I are totally planning to win this competition, so you might as well not even try. I'm just sayin'." She flipped her glossy hair over her shoulder and headed back to her pink boat.

I hoped their camp was far, far away from ours. I'm just sayin'.

We stood on the riverbank for what seemed like forever, waiting for the crew to shoot us getting into our boats to begin our journey downriver.

The sun was scorching hot by then. Wolf Adams stripped off his jungle jacket and hung it on a branch by the water. As he wandered away, my eye went straight to the pocket with my remote control. The cameras weren't rolling. It was my big chance.

"I'm going to get the remote," I whispered to Florida.

"Why? We're not going anywhere. Honey, do you know how many fabulous things I can buy for myself with a million dollars? And your Grandpa Jack won't have a single itty bitty thing he can say about the matter."

"Then I'll get it just in case. I mean if there's an emergency or something." Personally I thought that very moment counted as an emergency. My plan was to snatch the remote control and zap us out of there even if Florida was kicking and screaming.

"Oh, for heavens sake. Just hurry up." Florida went cross-eyed as she flicked a giant turquoise fly off her nose.

Not a soul was by the tree. Or so I thought. I made a dash for the jacket. I wasn't more than three feet away when that same wiry white-bellied eavesdropping spider monkey scrambled down the branches. He snatched the jacket and flung it as if it were a Frisbee, straight into the water. It floated down river and out of sight. I couldn't believe it! The remote control for the MegaPix 6000 was now somewhere in the Amazon River.

We were doomed.

Chapter Twenty-Nine

Florida had never paddled a canoe in her life. We drifted left to right, zigzagging back and forth past rickety raised huts perched high on the riverbank. I tried my best to keep us in a straight line, but Florida dragged her paddle in the water, steering us off course. The cameraman who was assigned to follow us in another canoe thought it was the funniest sight he'd ever seen. But I didn't.

"For the love of Pete, they gave us a defective boat! We'll never get to our base camp at this rate." Florida smacked her paddle in the water.

"Uh, I don't think it's the boat's problem. Try holding the top of the handle with one hand, and put your other hand down near the paddle blade. Then use long strokes." I demonstrated, pulling my own paddle through the water.

"And when did you become such an expert in water sports, young lady?"

"Mom taught me. We canoed or kayaked almost every weekend."

Florida sighed. "I never did understand that daughter of mine. How did she turn out to be so outdoorsy? There wasn't a girly bone in her body. If I hadn't been the only mother giving birth in the hospital that day, I'd have sworn they'd given me the wrong baby."

I couldn't believe my grandmother had said something so horrible. Maybe she was even a little surprised herself. She stopped paddling altogether and got real quiet. Maybe it had finally dawned on her that there were way worse things than having a daughter who wasn't a girly-girl. Like having a daughter who's dead, for starters.

At that moment I missed my mom even more. This river was just like the place I'd imagined her to be on her "extended vacation." Maybe I'd spot her around the next bend in our old yellow kayak. She would then magically whisk us both home to Bainbridge Island. But deep in my heart I knew it was just my own made-up fairy tale. My mom wasn't around the river bend. And no matter how much I wished it, she wouldn't be showing up to take me home.

It was five months, eleven days, and counting.

I shifted my thoughts to a vision of my mom watching me from some far-off place, maybe from high up in a cloud. I imagined she was proud that I was paddling just the way she'd taught me.

And just as she'd taught me, I paddled straight and true. But because it was only me doing the work, we were a whole lot slower than the other teams.

Before long, all signs of civilization disappeared. We were so deep in the jungle that no human dared to call it home.

Treetops poked up through the water as if whole sections of the forest had been flooded. The river was carpeted with humongous lily pads, big as umbrellas.

It was peaceful, but it wasn't quiet. There must have been a bazillion frogs croaking and dragonflies buzzing. Bright blue and yellow macaws squawked from the treetops. Was it a warning for us to turn back?

Then we heard the sound of a scary howling wind, except the air was still. Florida sat up at attention, and I admit it gave me the shivers.

"Lions. We're under attack!" Florida dove for the bottom of the boat.

"Lions don't live in South America," I said. "They're only in Africa."

Florida hoisted herself back onto the metal bench.

"Well, aren't we little Miss Smartypants? Maybe we should magically get you to be a contestant on *Jeopardy.*"

"No, thanks," I told her. Then I whispered that we probably shouldn't talk about our magic TV, especially in front of the cameraman who was videotaping us the whole time.

Not to mention that I'd promised Rosalie Claire I would never go into the TV again as long as I lived. And here I was, zapped into a reality TV show, paddling down a river in the Amazon rainforest. With scary noises roaring in the dark jungle.

Rosalie Claire. I missed her almost as much as I missed my mom.

Florida gave up paddling altogether. She lay back in the boat, using the collar of her lifejacket as a cushy pillow. Her hands hugged her knees while she watched me paddle.

"Could you speed it up a little, honey? We haven't seen the others for ages. Don't forget we're on a mission to make a million dollars."

"I'm going as fast as I can." But I don't think she believed me. The farther behind we got, the crankier she became.

"Okay," she finally said. "Teach me how to make this thing go."

I demonstrated one more time, and it wasn't long before Florida got the hang of it. We paddled together and picked up speed.

We kept looking for a red flag on the riverbank where we were supposed to get out and tie up our boat. Then we needed to follow the map inland to our base camp.

It felt as if we'd been paddling for hours, but I couldn't be sure. My arms were super-tired. For the longest time we didn't see anyone from the other teams, but eventually we passed the Blue Team—Victor and his mother, Carmen. Carmen was paddling, and Victor was hunched over his Gameboy.

"¡Dios mio, Victor! How you snuck that thing all the way here is beyond me. Careful or they'll take it away from you. If only I knew what went on in that thick head of yours. We'll be lucky if they don't kick us off the show!"

"Whatever," said Victor.

"Victor Antonio Gomez, don't you 'whatever' me. Remember the whole point of doing this? To get you away from computer screens and to make a man out of you. So pull it together, *mi hijo,* because this is the easy part."

"Whatever," said Victor.

His mother whacked at the water with her paddle. As we glided past them I heard noisy electronic music. It sounded like Victor's Pokémon was about to go into battle.

Okay, here's the thing. I agreed it was kind of dumb to play a Gameboy in the middle of the jungle. But the kid couldn't have been more than thirteen, and his mom wanted to turn him into a *man?* That seemed even dumber.

"Of all the nerve! They let that pimply boy bring his little video game and they took away our remote? That's hardly fair," Florida complained after we passed them by.

"He sneaked it. We got caught," I reminded her.

"Details, details."

"Well, the remote's gone now." I told her about the thieving monkey.

"Easy come, easy go," she shrugged. "Who needs it? We're here to win that money. Although I must say all this paddling nonsense is causing me to work up an unsightly sweat. Thank goodness I squirted on a little extra Jungle Gardenia today. I can almost smell it through the horrifying stench of that bug spray."

Within a couple of days everyone, including Florida, would probably think bug spray smelled pretty good compared to what we were all going to smell like—dirty, stinky, and gross.

I decided not to tell her what I was really thinking. Even if we stayed all fifteen days and won the money, we might not be able to get back home without that remote control.

Eventually, we passed a green flag on the riverbank and saw the green canoe tethered there. That meant Noah and Kevin were already on their way to their base camp. Around the bend, Florida spotted our red flag.

"Finally! We've reached our little home away from home!" she exclaimed.

"I think we have to find it first," I said.

"For heaven's sake, how hard could that be?"

Pretty hard, as it turned out.

Chapter Thirty

We dragged our red canoe up onto a sandbar and roped it to a tree. Now Florida insisted on navigating. She claimed she was born with a natural sense of direction.

I should have been suspicious. According to Grandpa Jack, other than the El Paso Airport, she'd never navigated anywhere outside of T or C.

I wore the backpack and lugged the machete. She carried the map. The cameraman and his assistant followed from behind.

On an overgrown path, we hiked deep into the jungle over a carpet of dead leaves, then turned left at a tree that was as tall as a skyscraper and as wide as Grandpa's pickup. Then the trail disappeared.

Using the machete, I chopped our way through bushes, branches, and vines. The whole time, Florida screeched, shrieked, and complained about the bugs. We stepped over armies of enormous ants and dodged moths as big as bear's paws. Insects flew everywhere—in our ears, down our shirts, even right up Florida's nose.

She screamed so loudly it probably scared every animal in the rainforest. Then she sneezed, snorted, and blew out a limp green dragonfly dripping with snot.

"You may not, under any circumstances, show that on TV," she instructed the cameraman.

He shrugged and smiled, which probably meant that was exactly what they would show.

Late in the afternoon, Florida admitted we were lost. We rechecked the map and realized she'd been holding it upside down. We retraced our steps, looking for all the piles of branches and vines I'd chopped down along the way.

Finally we found the right trail, crossed a river by leaping from log to log, and came upon a beautiful lake surrounded by bright green ferns. On the far side of the water I spotted a red flag staked not far from the shore. At last, our base camp.

"Ooh, time to freshen up," Florida exclaimed. "I'm hoping the place where we're staying has a nice big bathtub."

I should have warned her right then that we'd be roughing it, but she'd find out for herself soon enough.

By the way, it turned out it wasn't just *our* base camp. Everyone else was there too. By then, even Victor and Carmen had finished setting up their sleeping quarters. Our spot was right next to Jenna's campsite. Just my luck.

"We're *camping*?" Florida was in a state of shock. "As in *outside*?"

"They don't make it easy to win all that money. Besides, it's fun. Mom used to take me camping at the beach every summer."

"Of course she did. But I am not your mother. I don't camp."

"There's a first time for everything."

Florida leaned over and whispered in my ear. "Where are the bathrooms?"

"Behind the bushes, I guess."

"You have got to be kidding me! That's just *unnatural*." She wasn't whispering anymore. She was so loud that everybody looked over. Wolf Adams, who was relaxing in a folding chair, clamped his hand over his mouth trying his hide his laugh.

It was going to be an extremely long fifteen days.

While the other teams rested in their hammocks, Florida and I got to work. The campsites were pretty bare-bones. We had two hammocks, a couple of light blankets, a whole lot of mosquito netting, plus a tarp. We'd need to attach the tarp to the trees overhead to keep us dry in case it rained.

Even though I'd camped a bunch of times, my mom had always been in charge of knot-tying. I'd never learned how to do the fancy ones. So I attached the hammocks to the trunks of the trees with big double bows like the ones I always made when I didn't want my soccer shoes to come undone.

Well, double bows may work great on shoes, but they do not work great on hammocks. When we were done I crawled into mine to test it out. The hammock immediately crashed down to the jungle floor, with me in it.

It didn't hurt much, but I wanted to scream in frustration. The cameraman caught every second of it on videotape.

Jenna laughed out loud. "Geez, what a doofus," she muttered.

I swear I saw Wolf Adams wink at her, sharing the joke.

"All I know is I am *not* sleeping on the ground," said Florida.

"Good idea. Not unless you want the snakes to crawl under your covers in the middle of the night. Here, I can help."

It was the boy from the Green Team. Noah. He looked like he was about twelve. He had a nice smile and messy brown hair that flopped over one eye.

Noah helped me string up the hammocks and taught me to tie a proper knot. He called it a Double Double Dragon.

"Where did you learn to do that?" I asked.

He shrugged. "My dad and I camp in the summers to save money on rent. Turned me into a knot expert."

"Where do you live when you go to school?"

"Different places. Wherever my dad can get the best deal on an apartment. I've gone to eight different schools in eight years. It isn't the best, but I'm used to it by now."

It sounded to me like Noah and his dad could really use that million dollars.

We worked together to stretch our tarp above the hammocks. I shimmied up the tree, and Noah tossed me the rope. I fastened all four corners to the branches. Then I tried out my hammock. My Double Double Dragon knots held tight.

When we finished we didn't have a moment to rest. It was time for our first challenge.

Chapter Thirty-One

"Your challenge tonight," said Wolf Adams, "will be to collect enough dry wood to make a fire and boil your drinking water to kill off the parasites. Then you can relax, because tomorrow the real competition begins."

He handed each team a small crate. Florida and I pried ours open. Inside was a large cooking pot, a box of matches, and two energy bars. After all that hard work we weren't going to be eating much of a dinner. We'd be so hungry by the next morning we'd probably be ready to eat anything. That worried me.

"Oh come on, can't they even give a lady a mirror?" Florida was becoming more upset by the minute.

But it was a good thing there wasn't a mirror or Florida would have freaked out. In addition to her raccoon eyes, her fiery red hair was sticking out everywhere as if she'd stuck her finger in a light socket.

At the bottom of the box I found our "bathroom"—a roll of toilet paper and a small shovel.

• • •

We set out into the jungle with our machete to search for firewood. With all the dead wood around you'd think it would have been easy, but it turns out that the rainforest is wet. Super-wet. Luckily I knew just what to do because my mom and I used to camp in the soggy northwest. Instead of foraging for wood on the damp ground, I snapped dry twigs from trees, just the way she'd taught me. We didn't wind up with a lot. Just enough for one night with a little left over for the next day.

Jenna and her dad were the only ones back at base camp when we returned with our small stash. Their pile of wood was almost as big as a haystack.

"Wow, that's impressive!" I couldn't imagine how they'd done it.

"Just lucky. Looks like you guys are going to have a wimpy little fire. Too bad you didn't find much." Her lips pulled into a tight phony smile.

"We found enough." Jenna was getting on my nerves.

Before we could build a fire we needed rocks. Florida was reluctant to come with me until I reminded her of the million dollars, and she sprang to her feet. We found a scattering of small boulders at the edge of the lake. Together we rolled them back to our campsite and into a circle that became our fire ring.

"If Patsy could see me now, she would not believe her eyes," she said, wiping her dirty hands onto her pants.

My grandmother was 100 percent right about that. I could hardly believe it myself either.

With the firewood I built a teepee shape over a handful of kindling in the middle of the fire ring.

"I suppose your mother taught you that too?" Florida asked.

"Yep. She knew how to do a lot of stuff."

"Apparently. Maybe I shouldn't have complained so much about those camping trips she and your Grandpa Jack used to take. It appears they actually paid off."

Meanwhile, Jenna and her dad tried to light a pile of their wood, but their fire kept going out. They must've gone through at least half of their matches.

When I struck my first match and touched it to the kindling, I held my breath and hoped for the best. The tiny twigs smoldered, smoked, and began to crackle. Yes! Our log teepee burned hot and bright.

"That's a million-dollar fire, if I ever saw one," declared Florida.

Jenna glared at us.

The Green and Blue teams had returned and were busy building their own campfires. Noah and his dad worked to construct a pyramid shape with their wood. Victor's mother, Carmen, sat on a fallen log and barked orders like an army sergeant.

"You're doing it all wrong," she snapped.

"Whatever," said Victor.

It made me glad that at least Florida had helped out.

My grandmother and I carried our pot to the lake and filled it up. We needed to boil the water before we could drink it. We definitely didn't want to get parasites. It was gross enough to have all those bugs crawling around outside our bodies. Having them crawl around *inside* would have been triple gross, not to mention unhealthy.

When we returned I couldn't believe my eyes. Jenna had stuck a long stick into the middle of our campfire. When the end of it blazed she marched back to her haystack of wood and used it like a giant match. Her woodpile smoked and ignited. She had stolen our fire!

Violet would have been so mad if she'd seen Jenna do that. And boy, it made me mad too. Super-mad. Right then I decided I wanted to beat her in this competition.

"We should report her!" Florida was so angry that her face matched her hair.

But we didn't have to say a word. The cameras had caught her every move.

We settled in by our campfire and ate our energy bars. Our water was bubbling-hot when Noah and his dad came over. His dad, Kevin, carried their backpack. He zipped open the outer pouch and hundreds of fat ruby red berries spilled onto the ground.

"Hungry?" Noah asked. "We found these growing on the other side of the pond. They're called yumanasa berries."

Those yumanasa berries were the most delicious things I've tasted in my life and not because my stomach was growling. They reminded me of strawberries and sunshine. They almost made me forget how mad I was at Jenna.

"Why are you guys so buddy-buddy?" Jenna stared down at us with her hands on her hips. "We're not here to make friends, you know."

"We're not here to steal from each other either," I said.

"You don't know how it works, do you? The nastier you are, the more camera time you get."

At that moment, two cameras were recording every word.

Chapter Thirty-Two

"Are you people completely insane? Don't you know a lady needs her beauty sleep?"

I cracked open an eye. Florida was hidden beneath a thin blanket in her hammock as the camera crew recorded her tantrum on videotape.

"Cut! We're going to have to do this again!" It was the director, all covered up in his mosquito netting.

Okay, I admit it hadn't been the easiest night. It had been hard enough falling asleep in the first place with a blaring backdrop of jungle sounds. I'd expected to hear the dings and beeps of Victor's Gameboy, but at least that was silent. Maybe the batteries had died, or they'd taken it away from him.

Once I'd finally slipped into a dream, I was jolted awake by rain so ferocious that it sounded like baseballs attacking our tarp overhead.

"It sure isn't easy to make a million dollars," moaned Florida, before falling back to sleep.

Just before dawn, when the rain died down and I'd finally gone back to sleep myself, another noise awakened us. It was that scary howling racket we'd heard the day before on the river.

"Maybe it's a *South American* lion," Florida squeaked before burrowing under her blanket.

"No such thing," I said.

But the bellowing sound spooked me too. I decided to investigate.

I rolled out of my hammock and crept into the open. With dawn just breaking, I could barely make out the scene on the far side of the lake. And it wasn't scary at all. A yowling family of howler monkeys paced on the shoreline, making sure everyone in the rainforest was wide-awake. Guess those rackety monkeys were the Amazon's self-appointed alarm clocks. With all the moaning and groaning I heard behind me, it was obvious they'd woken up every single person in our campsite.

"Well, at least I won't be devoured by lions," Florida sighed when I reported back.

I'd just fallen back to sleep yet again when my grandmother's hollering woke me up for good.

"Okay, Florida. Come out from under the blanket. You're going to have to pretend to be asleep and then wake up. Then we'd like you to say, 'It wasn't exactly like staying in a Hilton Hotel.'"

"I need to brush my hair first." Florida's voice was muffled under the blanket.

"I'm sorry. We can't let you do that," said the director.

"Then you can't show me on your little TV show."

"I'm sorry, but we can." He sounded irritated.

"Can't."

"Can."

"Find me a hairbrush or I refuse."

"She's serious," I said. "I'd listen to her if I were you."

The director's face turned fire-engine-red and ropy veins stuck out on his forehead. He looked like he was ready to explode. But he dug into his pocket, pulled out his comb, and poked it through a slit in his netting.

"You win. This will have to do," he said.

Florida's arm sprang out from under her blanket, and she snatched the comb. "Thank you. Now will you please turn around and give a lady a minute to pull herself together?"

They turned their backs, and she sat up, ran the comb through her hair, fluffed it with her fingers, and then pinched her cheeks for color.

"Okay, boys. What is it you wanted me to say?"

Then they shot Florida and me pretending to be asleep and waking up. She said every single word that they wanted her to. So much for reality television being real. And by the way, Florida refused to give the director back his comb.

Chapter Thirty-Three

The time had come for our first big competition. Wolf Adams called it "Amazon Delicacies and Delights."

"Who here is hungry after a long hard day yesterday?" he asked us.

Everyone's hand shot up except for Victor's until his mother kicked him hard in the shin. I was so hungry that my stomach growled, but I wasn't looking forward to hearing the menu. I knew what they made people eat on this show.

"Now that you've all settled into your home away from home, it's time for breakfast," Wolf said to the camera, but his message was meant for us.

"I do hope you're about to serve us a great big platter of bacon and eggs." Florida smiled her 1,000-watt movie star smile. Maybe she thought she'd be able to flirt her way to a decent breakfast.

"Bacon and eggs?" I could tell he was amused. "No, Florida, we've got something entirely different in mind."

Then he turned and talked into the camera. "The Amazon abounds with food if you have the tools to fish and a keen eye for all the exotic fruits that grow here. So today's breakfast will be fish that you catch from the river and fruit that you pick from the aguaje palm tree. The team that returns first will earn a reward—an ice cold, two-foot high hot fudge sundae."

Fish and fruit for breakfast? That sounded great to me. And the sundae sounded amazing. The air was already thick and warm. Judging by everyone else's expressions, it looked like the other contestants were excited too.

Before he sent us off on our mission, Wolf Adams showed us a sample of an aguaje fruit. It was small, brown and scaly, about the size of a tangerine.

"Aguajes grow everywhere in the rainforest. The trick will be finding a tree that is short enough so you can reach the fruit. It is so delicious that in the towns and cities across Peru they make its juice into popsicles. Women swear that it makes them more beautiful."

Florida liked that part. A grin spread across her face. But I knew there had to be a catch. There always was.

"But here's the catch . . ."

See?

"In order to fish you'll need a fishing pole and a hook. We have that here for you." He held up a hooked fishing line, strung to a long skinny pole.

"And we even have bait." He opened his hand. On his palm wriggled a half dozen light brown fat wormy things, each about the size of my thumb.

"But you're going to have to earn it. Each one of you will have to eat six of these living, squirming Suri grubs in order to earn six more that you'll use for bait to catch your fish."

Everybody groaned. Even the camera guys made faces of disgust. Only Wolf Adams smiled. Of course he did. He didn't have to eat them.

I glanced at Florida. She looked like she was going to puke. It *was* a lot to have to put up with, just to try to win a hot fudge sundae.

We drew straws. The Blue Team went first. Carmen scrunched up her nose and popped all six of those fat wriggling creatures into her mouth at once. Her cheeks ballooned out like a Puffer fish as she mashed them with her molars.

When it was Victor's turn he refused to open his mouth. Then Carmen whispered something in his ear. Maybe she told him she'd crush his Gameboy. Victor said, "Whatever," but he ate them one by one, inspecting each wriggling grub closely before popping it in his mouth and gagging it down. When he was done, he coughed so hard I thought maybe one was stuck in his throat. But they earned their six grubs for bait and their fishing gear.

It was our turn next. Florida nudged me to go first. Wolf Adams put the six fat wriggly grubs in my hand and I stared down at them. I'd never ever eaten anything alive before. The thought was so disgusting that I worried I couldn't do it.

Then I noticed Jenna watching me. A smirk spread across her face. I couldn't chicken out and give her the satisfaction of seeing me fail.

I took a deep breath, popped one in my mouth and chomped down hard. It squished. It was crunchy on the outside and super-gooey on the inside. But here's the weird thing. The *idea* of eating grubs turned out to be worse than the taste. They reminded me of oysters. And I happen to like oysters. You might think it's strange that a kid who's only eleven likes oysters, but my mom and I used to harvest them on the beach, then eat them for dinner. So I pretended I was eating oysters. One by one I polished them off.

"Not so bad," I shrugged.

Jenna made a face at me.

Then it was Florida's turn. Maybe because she had her eye on all that money, or maybe because she knew she was on television, she pretended to be excited.

"I'm ready, Wolf." She smiled and stuck out her hand. He piled the grubs on her flattened palm. She studied them for a split second.

"Say goodnight, boys. You're about to become gourmet appetizers!" Then one by one she ate them like they were candy.

"Mmm! Scrumptious! Even better than bacon and eggs!" She licked her lips, as if she relished every bit of salty goo.

Wolf Adams looked shocked.

"Cut!" yelled the director through his gauzy net. The cameras shut off.

"Well, that *is* a surprise, Florida," said Wolf Adams. "We'll have to shoot that again, only this time pretend you can't stand them. Let's see you act like they're the worst things you've ever eaten in your life."

"They *are* the worst things I've eaten in my life and if you think I'm going to stick six more of those slimy, disgusting creatures down my throat you've got another think coming, Mister. I'm on a mission to win that money, and I'm playing my cards the way I see fit!"

Wow. My grandmother had turned out to be a great actress.

Since there was no arguing with Florida, they gave up and awarded us our fishing pole and bait.

It was the Pink Team's turn. Jenna narrowed her eyes at me. She turned to the camera with a big fake smile and volunteered to go first. It was obvious she wanted to show me up.

"These look so delicious! Almost as good as an ice cream sundae." The whole time she chewed she kept saying, "Yum! Yummy! Mmm!" It was as if she was copying Florida, but her face told a different story. You could see she hated it 100 percent.

Her dad downed them all fast. "Let's just say I wouldn't order them in a five-star restaurant."

When it was the Green Team's turn I wasn't surprised that both Noah and his dad, Kevin, ate them without a complaint.

"Not the best breakfast I've had, but not the worst," said Kevin.

"Not too bad. Tastes like oysters," said Noah.

I sure could relate to that kid.

Chapter Thirty-Four

Competition Number One was officially on. Florida and I took off on our search for aguajes. I was determined to fill up our backpack with both fruit and fish and then be the first team to make it back to camp. I really wanted to win that sundae.

It turned out there were gazillions of aguaje trees in the rainforest. (In case you didn't know, this is how you pronounce it: ah-GWA-hey). And Wolf Adams wasn't joking about them being tall. The giant palm trees stretched at least 100 feet into the sky. There was no way we could climb to the top to pick the fruit.

I wished I'd had Rosalie Claire's magic pouch. Inside I'd probably find it jam-packed with those scaly fruits.

Where were we going to find fruit low enough to the ground that we could pick?

Then I remembered. When we were lost and trying to find our camp, there was a tree that looked just like an aguaje but it was a whole lot shorter. Florida and I retraced our steps from the day before, hiking the trail I'd cleared with the machete.

We finally came to an opening, and there was the tree. It wasn't much taller than a house and it was dripping with long clusters of fruit that nearly touched the ground. Aguajes! The camera guy videotaped us filling our backpack with fruit.

We were one step closer to ice cream. It was time to go fishing.

The camera guy followed us to the spot on the river where we'd tied up our boat. It looked like a good enough place to fish. Not that I'm an expert or anything. But it was hard to miss the scads of fish swishing back and forth beneath the water's surface.

We settled onto the bank in the shade. Dozens of turtles skittered out of our way, splashing into the river. I pulled out our fishing gear.

Our cameraman excused himself and promised he'd be right back. He said he'd used his last videocassette and needed to grab another one. I was relieved. For at least a little while I wouldn't have a camera recording my every move.

The Suri grub wriggled and squirmed as I carefully threaded it through the hook, just the way Rosalie Claire had taught me.

"Honey, I'm sure glad you know how to do that. The only fish I know how to catch are the breaded fish sticks in the frozen food section at the Shur-Sav. Glad you won't need my help on this one."

I told her I could handle it. Florida got busy swatting bugs from her arms and legs while I cast the line into the water and waited for a bite.

I waited, and waited, and waited. I could see the fish. Dozens of fish. Great big ones. Over and over they bumped into my line, but not a single one took the bait. Then it came to me. Rosalie Claire had said to use yellow feathers for sunny weather and red feathers when it's cloudy. With all the shade on the bank of the river, I needed a red feather to make a fly that would attract the fish.

"I'll be right back," I told Florida. "I need to find something."

"Try to hurry, honey. These jungle sounds give me the willies."

"Don't worry. It's only howler monkeys and a bunch of yackety parrots."

Parrots. That was it! I'd follow the squawking of the parrots. I picked my way upriver, over fallen logs, tangled brush, and damp leaves. After a while I decided it would be easier to walk in the water. I moved down to the shallows of the riverbank and kept on. My shoes sloshed and the water felt cool squishing through my toes in the hot jungle. The parrots' racket grew louder.

I rounded the bend and spotted them—an enormous flock of parrots high in the trees. And I was in luck. They were bright red, yellow, and blue. Now I needed to find a feather on the ground. I poked around in the underbrush. It didn't take long to find a ruby-red feather. I slid it into my pocket.

Then I heard something horrifying. Someone was screaming in pain. It was Victor.

And even louder than Victor's howls were Carmen's shrieks. "*Oh mi dios,* Victor! Why on earth would you stick your finger in a piranha's mouth?"

Piranha!? The human-attacking fish? Here in the Amazon River? When we were in second grade, Violet and I watched them swim in a tank in the Seattle Aquarium. They swooshed right up to the glass baring their vicious teeth and looked like they wanted to chomp off our noses. It sent us running straight for the exit sign.

On the way back to our fishing spot I avoided walking in the water. The last thing I wanted was to be picked to the bone by a school of deadly piranhas.

Chapter Thirty-Five

Back at the fishing spot, Florida looked jittery as she swatted away dragonflies. I didn't tell her about the piranhas. It would only upset her.

"Thank goodness you weren't carried off by those nasty monkeys or attacked by wicked parrots."

Or devoured by bloodthirsty piranhas, I thought.

"I'm okay," I said.

For now.

I sat on the riverbank, plucked three long strands of hair from my head and braided them together to fashion a piece of string. I used the hair string to tie the red feather just above the hook. Then I slid another piece of grub bait onto the sharp curved tip and cast the line into the water.

The good news? The red feather worked its magic. In five seconds flat I felt a bite. The bad news? At the end of the line was a fourteen-inch piranha fish, its razor-sharp teeth clamped hard to the hook.

"Well, aren't you a wonder? It's a million dollar fishy!" At least my grandmother seemed proud of me. That was a plus.

But I still had the problem of getting the piranha off the hook. I kept thinking about Victor, so I decided to let the fish dangle on the end of the line until it gave its final breath. It flopped on the hook with its mouth gaping open, showing off white jagged teeth.

"My oh my, would you look at those chompers! If they aren't just like pointy thorns on a rosebush! Let's catch some more!" Florida handed me a grub.

"Uh, I think we only need to catch one." No way did I want to chance catching another killer fish. And as soon as this one died, I wanted to head straight back to camp. I was pretty sure we had a good chance of winning that sundae.

"How in the world do you know so much about fishing, honey? Is that something else Angela taught you?"

I wished my mom had taught me how to fish, but learning from Rosalie Claire was the next best thing. I thought about telling Florida the truth. After coming face-to-face with a real live piranha, nothing would ever seem as scary, especially the truth.

"Actually, Rosalie Claire taught me how to fish. She also taught my mom."

My grandmother's face bloomed redder than a radish.

"I have made my feelings about that woman very clear. She is a nutcase. And she's just as peculiar now as she was back in high school."

"What do you mean?"

"Her nose was always buried in some strange book. She didn't give half a hoot about doing anything that normal girls are supposed to do. Never wore a spot of makeup or a splash of perfume."

Reading books? No makeup? No perfume? Those seemed like reasonable choices to me.

"Are you sure that's really it?" I asked, knowing there must be a deeper reason.

We sat with silence hanging between us until Florida finally spoke. Her voice was quavery and filled to the brim with sadness.

"Maybe that's not it. Maybe the real reason is because she and her Grandma Daisy tried to steal your mother from me. When Angela was young, she would come up with every excuse under the sun to run next door. Sometimes I think those two women conspired to bewitch your mother into liking their company more than mine."

"She did like them, Florida, but you were still her mom. Kids love their moms," I said.

"I suppose so. But the truth is, I wasn't a very good one." Florida sighed and stared off at nothing in particular. "I sometimes think I just wasn't cut out to be a mother. Heck, I couldn't bake a batch of cookies to save my life."

"Being a mom isn't about baking cookies."

"Maybe not. But I was never good at any of it. Your mother and I bumped heads from the minute she was born. Anything I asked her to do, she'd turn around and do the opposite. She refused to spend time with the right girls. She hardly ever dated boys I approved of. I swear, she always had a mind of her own."

"Everyone has a mind of their own, or at least they should. That's what my mom always said."

Florida got all choked up. "Deep down maybe I've always known it wasn't really Rosalie Claire and Daisy who stole her away. It was me who let her go."

Tears spilled down my grandmother's cheeks. Then it hit me. Maybe all that sadness was why she bought so much stuff from the TV. It made her feel happy, if only for a little while.

Then she really started to cry. Big gasping sobs. "I never had a chance to tell your mother how sorry I was. And now it's too late."

My grandmother's sobs reminded me of all those times I'd cried after my mom died. Florida was finally, really and truly, missing her.

"Look at me," she finally said as she wiped away her tears. "I'm a mess! And I haven't touched up my makeup in over twenty-four hours."

"You're prettier this way," I told her. And it was true. She didn't have on a spot of makeup, and she might have looked a little older, but she looked a lot more beautiful.

"Thanks, honey. And you know what? I may have loused up things with your mother, but she did a decent job of raising you. Maybe I should be grateful she had Daisy and Rosalie Claire. You and your mother turned out all right, no thanks to me."

She draped her arm over my shoulder. It was the closest I'd ever felt to Florida.

The piranha I'd caught had finally given up the fight. Just like Rosalie Claire had taught me, I took one hand and grabbed the fish under its gills, then used the other hand to guide out the hook. We wrapped up our dead piranha in leaves the size of elephants' ears and slipped it into the backpack.

Florida and I headed up the trail toward camp. There was something that gnawed at me.

"Florida, did you ever know my dad?"

"Danny? He was the only boy I approved of. At first, anyway. He and Angela went to Hot Springs High together. After graduation she moved to San Francisco for college. Danny went to visit, and they got married. But they didn't invite Jack and me to the wedding. At the time, your mother and I weren't exactly on speaking terms."

"Do you know what happened to him?"

"I haven't a clue. When you were a baby your father just took off. He slipped a goodbye note under the door and was never heard from again. Didn't even contact his folks."

"Do they live near you?" It occurred to me that I might have a whole other set of grandparents living close by.

"No. They moved away years ago. I have no idea where they went."

"I sure wish I knew why he left."

Florida shrugged. "Who knows? I always thought he got into some nasty trouble. Maybe even died. Wish I had a better answer."

I'd always known my father's name, but that was all. My mother had never wanted to talk about him. It made her too upset, she'd said. Now at least I knew he'd also grown up in T or C. Perhaps even fished from the same pond where I caught my first trout. And maybe he'd even held my mom's hand as they walked down Main Street.

"But is it possible he's still alive?" I asked.

"Possible, but I doubt it. I mean, who drops off the face of the earth like that?"

I guess she was right. I just wished I knew for sure. But my mom always said that some things are meant to remain a mystery, and maybe this was one of them.

As Florida and I made our way around twisting vines and fallen logs, we came upon a curtain of multicolored butterflies. There must have been at least a thousand of them dancing back and forth in streams of sunlight. As we wove our way through the kaleidoscope of colors, dozens of butterflies fluttered and landed gently on our shoulders.

"Come on, honey. Let's go collect that sundae. We sure do deserve it," and Florida.

And she reached out to take my hand.

Chapter Thirty-Six

"You made it back faster than I thought." It was the camera guy, walking toward us on the path to our camp.

Fast? Really? He'd been gone for over an hour. I thought it was peculiar that he looked so surprised.

"Catch anything?" he asked.

"Yep," I said.

"Let's plan on staging another fishing expedition so I can grab some shots. We'll need them for the show."

Go fishing for another piranha? Not in a gazillion years.

It turned out we weren't the first ones who'd returned to camp with our fish and fruit. Guess who was? If you guessed Jenna and her dad, Rob, you are unfortunately absolutely 100 percent right. They had a tower of aguajes twice as high as ours, and a giant catfish.

"Look who didn't win the sundae," Jenna taunted. "Bet you're mad."

Mad? Not exactly. But I *was* disappointed. I didn't want to give her the satisfaction of knowing that, so I only shrugged.

I had begun to build a fire to cook our fish when the two other teams straggled in. Victor's piranha-bitten pointer finger was wrapped up tight in a fat white bandage. Both of the other teams had also caught fish, but they hadn't managed to find any low-hanging aguaje fruit. That made Jenna snicker.

"What's so funny?" I asked.

"Guess the other teams weren't smart enough to find the only short aguaje tree around here."

How in the heck did she know there was only one?

Since we had so many aguajes, I decided to share them with the Green and Blue teams.

"As long as you keep enough for me. I am dying to experience their legendary powers of beautification," said Florida.

Carmen's eyes narrowed into slits when I handed her a small pile. "Why are you giving us these? That's not how the game is played."

"That's how I play it," I told her. "We have more than we can eat."

"Hope they taste better than the grubs," said Victor. "Thanks."

"You're welcome," I said. Wow. It was the first time I'd heard Victor say anything other than "whatever."

I gave Noah and Kevin a half dozen of the fruits and invited them to join us at our campfire to cook their catch. They'd reeled in a bass nearly twice the size of our fish. I wished I'd been so lucky.

"Holy smokes, you caught yourself a piranha!" Noah whistled in admiration.

Florida's eyes shot open so wide I thought they'd pop from her head. "Piranha? You mean the fish that *eats* people?"

"In this case it looks like it's going to be the people eating the fish," smiled Noah. "It turns out this particular piranha had more to worry about than you did. Only the red-bellied ones are dangerous."

Our fish didn't have a speck of red on it. I wish I'd known that *before* I'd reeled it in.

Noah sliced open both fish and cleaned out the guts. We cooked and shared the piranha and the bass, fifty-fifty. They tasted delicious, maybe because they actually were or maybe because I was so hungry. Florida thought the piranha was so tasty she planned to ask the Shur-Sav to start carrying it at the fish counter.

Kevin scraped a sharp rock along the brown scales of the aguaje, stripping the hard skin from the fruit. Inside, it glistened buttery yellow. It was gooey in the center, with a cluster of three fat seeds. We all took bites and agreed it tasted like carrots.

"I do hope this little fruit gets busy working its beauty magic on me. Heaven knows I could use it right about now," Florida said as she ran her fingers through her hair.

Then she surprised me. She laughed. "Oh for heaven's sake, at this point I must resemble a complete and utter freak show. No makeup, no hairdo, and look at these nasty nails!" She presented her hands for inspection. "Caked with dirt, broken down to the quick, and barely a spot of polish left on them. I can't believe I'm saying this, but thank goodness I don't have a mirror!"

That's progress, I thought. The Amazon may have shown her another world, but deep inside, I suspected Florida was still Florida. She ate twice as many aguaje fruits as anyone else.

Wolf Adams presented Jenna and her dad with a hot fudge sundae that looked big enough for all four teams to share. But they didn't offer anyone a single bite. She and her dad dug in. Jenna made all kinds of happy slurpy noises probably just to rub it in our faces.

"Let Little Miss Nasty have her chocolate sundae," Florida said loud enough for all to hear. "It will surely cause her pretty complexion to break out in pimples, and it will make her fat." Then she turned and winked at the camera.

Jenna glared at Florida. After that she only picked at her sundae. Eventually it melted into a giant milky soup.

Chapter Thirty-Seven

I heard the scream not long after Florida and I crawled into our hammocks for a mid-day rest.

"Snake!!!"

Jenna stood paralyzed at the base of the tree that separated her campsite from ours. Her face was smeared with chocolate sauce. She stared dumbstruck into the branches. Peering right back at her was the longest snake I'd seen in my whole entire life. Way bigger than that rattler in Truth or Consequences. Its forked tongue flicked in and out of its open mouth. It had fangs four times the size of piranha teeth.

"Oh my goodness," gasped Florida. "Somebody do something!"

The camera crew was filming Victor and Carmen on the far side of camp, and everyone else was over there watching. The loudmouthed howler monkeys drowned out our yells for help.

I quivered with fear, but I knew what I had to do. "Back up slowly, Jenna," I said as I slid from my hammock.

The snake slithered toward her.

They were nearly nose-to-nose, the snake's flicking tongue practically licking the chocolate sauce from Jenna's cheek.

I seized our machete and quietly inched forward, trying not to crunch the leaves under my feet. The snake chose that moment to strike. It flew from the tree, slamming down on Jenna's right shoulder. Its weight pulled her hard to the ground. Jenna screamed. But the sound only blended into the howler monkeys' cries already filling the rainforest.

I lifted my machete.

The snake's mouth gaped wide, its poisonous fangs ready for the kill. With every ounce of strength, I crashed the sharp blade down on the snake's head, slicing it clean off with a single chop. I'd missed Jenna's shoulder by less than an inch.

Perhaps it was the shock of seeing a kid kill a snake, but the monkeys immediately hushed. The rainforest was dead silent.

I started to cry, and I'm not even sure why. Maybe it was because it was the most scared I've ever been, next to when my mom died. Maybe it was because the whole snake incident reminded me of Rosalie Claire, and I wished she'd been here to protect me. Maybe it was because I was only eleven and way too young to have just chopped up a giant snake all by myself. I turned away because I didn't want Jenna to see me crying, but she did.

"What are you bawling for?" Jenna snapped as she scrambled to her feet, pulling dead leaves from her hair. "I was the one who almost got killed."

I couldn't answer. All my words had flown away.

"Well, at least they didn't get any of that on camera. The last thing I need is to have people see you trying to save me."

"*Trying* to save you? You horrid little monster!" Florida was hopping mad. "She *did* save you! And you should be down on your bony little knees, kissing the toes of Madison's sneakers!"

Wow. Go, Florida! I'm not one for telling people off, but Jenna sure had it coming. You might think at that very moment I was sorry I'd saved her, but I wasn't. Not one bit. I don't care how much you dislike someone, it's wrong to wish for something super-bad to happen to them. And the best thing? It felt really good to have my grandmother stand up for me.

Florida's yelling brought everyone running. When Jenna's dad showed up, she instantly transformed into a damsel in distress. She dashed into his waiting arms.

Wolf Adams sauntered over, letting out a low drawn-out whistle. "Now that's impressive," he said.

He inspected the snake's impossibly long body. It was a deep walnut brown, patterned with coffee-colored diamonds. Heel to toe, heel to toe, he paced it off with his jungle boots.

"Would you look at that! We've got ourselves an eight-foot-long Fer-de-lance. The deadliest snake in the Amazon. What in the devil's name happened?"

Florida stepped forward. "I saw it all. But my lips are sealed until you turn on those cameras!"

Two cameras clicked on and she reported everything, even the part about Jenna being ungrateful.

Jenna's eyes narrowed. She wiped the chocolate from her face and marched right up to Florida, shoving her out of the way. Then she faced the cameras.

"That poor snake was minding its own business when Madison waved her machete at it. That's the reason it attacked. And you know why? She wanted to *make* it attack me so I'd have to leave the show. She's afraid I'll win!"

Then she turned to me and said, "F.Y.I., Madison McGee, you *should* be afraid. Very afraid!" She flounced off into the jungle with her dad trotting at her heels.

Chapter Thirty-Eight

The following morning, Wolf Adams gathered us all together at the crack of dawn to announce the next competition. Well, almost all of us. Jenna and her dad, Rob, were missing. Noah whispered that he'd seen them head out on a walk before sunrise. We had to stand around and wait until they finally strolled back to base camp. They didn't even apologize for being late.

When the cameras switched on, Wolf Adams switched on the charm. "For the people who live here in the rainforest, the Amazon River is both a challenge and a key to their survival. It provides food—and it provides a means of travel.

"Today you will all travel down the river once more—only this time your teams will be racing each other through a course we've set up. Forty colored flags have been planted in the water—ten for each team. Your goal is to paddle downriver, collecting your ten team flags along the way. The first team to cross the finish line with all ten of their flags will win a four-course steak dinner with all the trimmings."

"I need a real meal. Let's win this thing," said Florida as we lugged our backpacks down to the river.

It was the third day and everyone stank of sweat and morning breath. Well, everyone but Wolf Adams and the crew. I don't know where they disappeared to at night, but they always came back in the morning smelling of soap and minty aftershave.

As for me, I was hot, sticky, and dirty. I longed for my remote control. Zapping out of there was way more appealing than a river race, even if there was a chance to win a steak dinner. I decided it was far more fun to watch other people do this kind of stuff on TV than actually doing it yourself.

By the time we reached the river, clouds were forming overhead. At the time I was thankful because they blocked the sun and cooled off my skin.

Our metal canoes were lined up single file on the shore. Florida and I climbed into ours, me in the back and Florida in the front.

Jenna sauntered over and leaned in close.

"Want to know a secret?" she whispered.

"Maybe," I said, because I wasn't really sure I did.

"The producers want me to win."

"It doesn't work that way, Jenna. It's a competition."

"Go ahead and think that. All I want to say is don't try to 'save' me again." She used her fingers to make quotes in the air when she said the word "save." "I don't want you looking better than me and messing up my future. I'm just sayin'."

And I'm just sayin' Jenna was one of the meanest, nastiest kids I'd ever met. But I had to wonder. Was she telling the truth? Was the show really rigged? Or did she just want me to believe that? Didn't people in the audience have to call in and vote for a winner? I hoped she was only trying to scare me.

Everyone paddled into position side by side in the middle of the river. Colored flags zigzagged down the Amazon as far as I could see. Each one was attached to a buoy anchored to the depths of the riverbed. This time the camera guys were positioned on the shore, poised to catch shots of the teams as we passed by.

Noah and Kevin were on one side of us, Victor and Carmen on the other.

Victor splashed at the water with his paddle to get my attention. "Pssst. Watch out for Jenna. She's like Jessie in Team Rocket. She's out to get you. And your camera guy is helping her cheat," he whispered.

"Hush, Victor," said Carmen. "It's none of your business."

"Whatever."

Our camera guy? He must have been the one to show her the aguaje tree we'd found when he told us he needed to go back to get more videotape. It all made sense! I was burning mad.

Now the only thing I could think of was beating Jenna.

Wolf Adams pulled out his trumpet and played his horse race song again. We all started paddling hard.

"Good luck," Noah called to me.

"You too!"

I tried to concentrate on pulling my paddle fast through the water, but I kept thinking about what Victor had said. Our boat fell behind the pack.

"Speed it up!" yelled Florida. "There's a steak dinner and a million bucks on the line!"

"I don't care about that! I just want somebody to beat Jenna," I yelled back.

"Sounds good to me! And if somebody has to beat her it might as well be us!"

I'd never seen my grandmother work so hard. I was impressed. I picked up my pace, and we caught up to Victor and his mom. This time he was actually paddling.

"Is that the best you can do?" Carmen snapped at him.

"Yes it is, Mother. Deal with it!" Victor yelled back.

Good for you, Victor, I thought. I gave him the thumbs-up as we zipped by.

Florida and I quickly worked out a system. Whenever we'd come up on one of our flags, we'd paddle at top speed toward it. I'd keep us on course while she reached out and grabbed it.

She missed the second one so we had to backtrack upriver to get it. If you've never paddled against the current, let me tell you, it's hard work. Of course they caught it on camera. After that, Florida didn't miss a single flag.

We'd gathered five of our flags. Halfway there. When we rounded the bend, we caught sight of the Green and Pink Teams. The two boats were neck and neck, with Jenna and her dad slightly in the lead. The clouds in the sky were turning thick and grey as campfire smoke.

Florida snatched our sixth flag. Then I watched with dismay as Noah and Kevin's boat slammed into two boulders on the shore. They appeared to be safe but they were wedged in tight between the rocks. With their paddles they worked to free themselves. Jenna's boat shot into the lead.

"Need help?" I yelled as we raced toward their boat.

"No! We'll be fine! Just go get 'em!"

"We're on it!" I shouted.

I paddled faster than I ever believed was possible. My arms were so sore I thought they'd drop off, but I kept going. Finally our red metal canoe swept past their pink one. We were in first place.

That's when I noticed it. Our boat had sprung tiny leaks. Dozens of them. Little corks of debris popped up from what appeared to be small, freshly bored holes in the bottom of our canoe.

"Don't miss that red flag!"

"Forget the flags, Florida. Start bailing!" I shouted.

Florida was right on top of it. She threw down her paddle and bailed out water with her hands while I tried to steer us toward the riverbank.

The Pink Team's boat glided next to ours. "Oh, is your boat leaking? So sad. I wonder how in the world *that* happened? I simply can't imagine." Jenna's lips pulled into a tight super-satisfied smile.

Her dad kept his head down as if he was embarrassed to look at us. He paddled hard, and their canoe whizzed into first position.

So that was why Jenna and her dad had arrived late. They were busy poking holes in our boat and stuffing them with something they knew would disintegrate in the middle of the race. They were trying to eliminate us from the competition!

Then, believe it or not, things got worse. While I tried to paddle to the safety of the shore, the sky opened up, deluging us with a dense blanket of rain. We could barely see three feet ahead of us. The river transformed into the color of caramel sauce and churned with growing speed. Our canoe was filling up fast with murky brown water.

The banks overflowed, sending the camera guys scrambling into the forest. It was a flash flood! As we became hopelessly caught in the current, we lost control of the boat. Up ahead I could barely make out the pink canoe as it rammed into a log and capsized into the river. Jenna and Rob plunged into the Amazon. I caught glimpses of their bright pink bandanas bobbing up and down as they worked to keep their heads above the raging water.

"Help! Somebody please help!" they pleaded.

"All the money in the world isn't worth this! We're going to die!" yelled Florida.

"Not if I can help it! Just keep bailing! Use my shoe!" I yanked off a sneaker and tossed it to her. Florida frantically scooped out water as our boat barreled ahead.

I decided I had to try to save Jenna and her dad. I didn't care how nasty that girl was, or even that she'd told me not to save her. I couldn't let them drown. But our boat was taking on too much water. A swift-moving current swept us far away from them, far away from the watery racecourse, and shot us down a faster churning fork of the Amazon River. We were headed straight for a waterfall!

"We'll have to jump and swim to shore," I screamed.

"I can't swim!" Florida cried.

"You'll have to try!"

"I can't!"

"Hang onto me! We'll jump together!"

"Nobody's doing anything of the sort!"

I could hardly believe my ears and my eyes. I blinked hard, but there she was, as real as could be. Sitting in the middle of our canoe was Rosalie Claire. And she was holding the remote control for the MegaPix 6000!

"I finally found this darn thing and managed to get myself here," she shouted over the fury of the swirling river. "Madison, you're going to have to get us out!"

Florida looked like she'd just seen a ghost. "How in the world . . . ?"

"No time to explain!" I interrupted, dropping my paddle.

Rosalie Claire thrust the remote into my hands. I worked fast because we were hurtling toward the edge of the steep raging waterfall. I prayed that what I had in mind would work.

"Everyone hold hands!" I commanded. I held tight to Rosalie Claire and she reached for Florida. My grandmother hesitated then came to her senses. She clutched Rosalie Claire's hand like a life raft.

I balanced the remote on my lap. With my free hand I pressed the purple button and the silver return button at the same time. The noise of the waterfall was deafening. I couldn't hear if the remote pinged. But as our canoe catapulted over the waterfall, my blurry vision and the icy-cold lightning shooting through my body were unmistakable.

I drew my very next breath in Florida's living room. Rosalie Claire was right between my grandmother and me, gripping tightly onto our hands. Water from our bodies pooled on the tile floor around our feet.

The expression on Florida's face was priceless. She stared in amazement at Rosalie Claire. I don't think she'd ever been happier in her entire life to see another human being. And I can tell you for an absolute fact that neither had I.

Chapter Thirty-Nine

The three of us fell into one giant soaking-wet hug on the sofa. The red velvet cushions sponged up the murky water from the Amazon.

"You came back!" I snuggled close to Rosalie Claire.

"Of course I did. You needed me."

Leroy scratched at the sliding glass door. Florida said it was fine to let him in, since at the moment we were probably filthier than any dog could ever be.

Leroy grinned from ear to ear. He leaped into my arms and knocked me down flat, licking me from head to toe. I didn't mind a bit. I was just as happy to see him too.

"Good boy!" I told him. "I missed you!"

He worked off my soggy red bandana with his teeth and proceeded to shred it to bits.

"Leroy would have been a better boy if he hadn't buried your TV remote control in the backyard," Rosalie Claire said. "Or I could have rescued you a lot sooner."

So that's where the missing TV remote went!

"Not long after we pulled onto the highway I had a bad feeling in my gut. I made the Super Shuttle driver drop me off just north of Caballo Lake. My old boss from the retirement home picked me up and brought me back here. I was just in time to see the two of you traipsing through the rainforest on the TV. By the way, impressive job getting that fire started. I'm proud of you."

"Thanks," I said.

"I had a hunch there had to be a second remote around somewhere, since no self-respecting magic TV would come without a back up. I searched every nook and cranny, box, and drawer."

Given how many boxes were stacked and stashed around the house, I could only imagine how long it must have taken.

When she couldn't find it, Rosalie Claire admitted she was getting worried. It was a two-hour show, and the clock was ticking. Before she knew it we were climbing into our canoes for the river race.

"By the way, that girl Jenna—she is bad news," Rosalie Claire said.

"The worst," said Florida.

Rosalie Claire's lucky break—and, more to the point, *our* lucky break—was when she saw Leroy digging holes in the yard.

"Tipped off by my intuition," she said.

With her shovel she unearthed sticks, stones, bones and filthy old computer parts until she finally discovered the remote control—along with four pairs of my dirty socks.

"And Madison, thank goodness you'd told me how to use that thing, or I would still be trying to figure it out."

"And we would be at the bottom of a watery grave," said Florida.

"You're my hero," I told Rosalie Claire as I laid my head in her lap.

"I think you're *both* my heroes," said Florida.

Then together we all watched the rest of the *Stranded in the Amazon* episode.

Noah and Kevin managed to pull Jenna and Rob to safety. The pink canoe floated off with all their pink flags, never to be seen again. Once the rain stopped and the river slowed, Noah, Kevin, Jenna, and Rob piled into the green canoe and paddled back to base camp.

I'm absolutely sure that Wolf Adams had no idea what became of us. At the end of the episode he announced that Florida and I had to leave unexpectedly because of important "family business" and we weren't coming back. It would have been much cooler if he'd said we'd been zapped back to Truth or Consequences by a MegaPix 6000 remote control. But how could he have guessed that? And who would believe it, anyway?

They showed Victor and Carmen having a giant fight on the river. They never got close to finishing the race, and if you ask me, they were the lucky ones.

Florida and I decided that we'd send a note to the people at the show to let them know we hadn't plunged to our deaths down that waterfall.

A few weeks after the final episode aired, Noah sent me a newspaper article that exposed the producers. They really did try to rig it so Jenna would win. Her dad had made a secret deal with them—if the pink team won, they wouldn't take a penny of the million dollars, and the producers would keep it for themselves. In exchange, Jenna would get her own TV show. So I guess Jenna was kind of telling the truth about that part all along. But in the end, Noah and his dad won the million dollars. Noah called me later to tell me they used some of the money to buy their very first house.

When the credits rolled I leaned over, picked up the remote control and put the MegaPix on mute.

That's when Florida noticed my Firebird necklace. I'd kept it safely tucked inside the neck of my T-shirt the whole time we were in the Amazon. When Leroy bowled me over with his licking, he must have pulled it free.

"My goodness! Your mother had a necklace just like that. Is that hers?"

I traded looks with Rosalie Claire, and she nodded to me. This was my story to tell.

"It was a present from Rosalie Claire before she left for the airport.

It's just like the one she gave Mom when she was a kid." I held the charm in my hand. It was the link that tied together my mother, Rosalie Claire, and me.

"Just a small token to remind Madison how important it is to spread her wings," Rosalie Claire told Florida.

"It's beautiful," said Florida.

"Thank you," Rosalie Claire and I said in unison.

"Now Madison has something to remember me by," she added.

Then it struck me. Rosalie Claire was still leaving.

I choked back my tears. "I wish you weren't going."

She slipped her arm around me. "I have to, you know."

"Your destiny," I said, and rested my head on her shoulder.

"Maybe you can visit," said Florida. "If it's all right with Rosalie Claire."

"There's nothing I would love more," Rosalie Claire said.

"Me too," I said.

"You know what, honey?" said Florida. "If I sell off some of my shopping show stuff I could buy you a plane ticket. Maybe you can go down there next month before school starts."

A funny look came over Rosalie Claire. She unzipped her fanny pack, and her lips curled into a knowing smile. "You won't have to sell off a thing if you don't want to, Florida. Looks like my fanny pack has plans for Madison." She fished out an envelope and waved it in the air. "I just found a plane ticket. Can you come for two weeks in August?"

Just like always, Rosalie Claire's magic fanny pack had exactly what I needed. I looked at Florida with my most hopeful expression and crossed my fingers for luck.

"Of course she can," said Florida.

I threw my arms around my grandmother's neck, and for the first time she didn't pull away. Then she did something amazing. She opened up her arms and pulled Rosalie Claire right into our hug. Only a couple of hours ago she would have thrown a hissy fit if Rosalie Claire had even walked into our house, but so much had changed. Florida finally saw Rosalie Claire for who she was, not who she imagined her to be.

A few hours before, there was nothing in the world I wanted to do more than to fly away with Rosalie Claire—and far, far away from Florida. But something had changed in me too. I was ready to give my grandmother a second chance.

Later that night when the Super Shuttle honked its horn, we all hugged goodbye. Florida even blew Rosalie Claire a kiss.

My grandmother and I sat together on the sofa, still filthy, but at least we were finally dry. Leroy snored by my feet. An old black-and-white movie played on the muted TV.

"Well, we didn't win the million dollars," sighed Florida as I watched the MegaPix light flicker on her face.

"I never thought we would," I said.

"Maybe I could make a million if I sold off all of this stuff of mine."

"A million might be a stretch."

"I suppose, but it's worth a try. And the first thing I'm going to do? Get rid of this magic TV. Then maybe your grandpa would have me back."

"That's worth way more than a million dollars," I told her.

"I think you're right."

Then my grandmother picked up the remote control and switched off the MegaPix 6000 for the last time.

Chapter Forty

Early the next morning, I dug the MegaPix contract out from the bottom of my underwear drawer and read the fine print.

> *The manufacturers of the MegaPix 6000 are not responsible for any bodily injury to a viewer or death that might result from teleporting into the television.*

Boy, I sure wished I'd read that *before* stuffing it in with my underwear. I kept on reading:

> *The return of the MegaPix 6000 is only permitted if the buyer has activated the teleportation feature on at least one occasion.*

No problem there. I'd been zapped, or teleported, *three* times. At the bottom of the contract was a phone number. Florida called it.

Mike answered the phone, and Florida told him she was done with the TV. He said he was happy to hear it and impressed we'd made it out of the Amazon alive. Sounded like he'd been watching us the whole time.

The following day the MIRACLE MOVERS truck pulled up to the house. The bell rang and I answered.

"Hey Squirt, we're here to pick up the MegaPix."

"Thank goodness," I said.

"You had yourself quite an adventure or three," he said as he and his partner with the pimples packed up the TV. "I gotta say, Squirt, you're one impressive kid."

"Thanks. It turned out to be a summer I never in a million years could have imagined."

They were done packing up when Mike noticed there was only one remote. I told him the other one was probably somewhere on the bottom of the Amazon River.

"Ooh. We don't have another one. It was just the two. That'll make it real interesting for the dude in New York City who's getting this contraption next."

I wondered what adventures the MegaPix would deliver to the unsuspecting guy in New York.

As they headed back to the truck, a strange feeling came over me. I ran outside after them. There was something I needed to ask.

"Mike, how does it all work? The magic, I mean."

"What do *you* think it is?" he asked.

Only one thing made sense. "I think it's kind of like my friend Rosalie Claire's pouch. It's the magic that gives you what you need when you need it. At least, that's how it worked for me with the MegaPix."

"Exactly."

One more question itched at me. "How did you know we needed that TV?"

"I can't take all the credit. This may sound hard to believe, but it was your mom. She was the one who told me. Well, she didn't tell me, *exactly*. We magic folks know how to read the messages up in the clouds. And not too long ago, when I was watching them change shape, I got a feeling she was telling me you needed a little magic. I thought the MegaPix might just do the trick."

"But my mom never believed in magic."

"Did you ever think maybe she knew more about it than she let on?"

My mom? I couldn't believe it! Or maybe I could. Thinking back, I remembered that, whenever the subject of magic came up, she'd clam up and look like she was holding onto some deep, sad secret. Maybe someday I'll know why, but today I was just happy to know that my mom believed in magic, just like me. And I was even happier to know that all along she really *was* watching over me. Maybe I even knew it that day when I spied the angel up in the clouds.

I thought of Mom's spirit floating somewhere high in the sky. I realized she helped me to understand that life can actually get good again. Now I know it just gets good in a new way.

Mike winked at me as he and his partner got into the truck. I watched it backfire and bounce as it drove away. There was no way that bucket of bolts was going to make it all the way to New York City. And I wasn't at all surprised at what happened next. When it was halfway down the street, the MIRACLE MOVERS truck turned all shimmery and wavy like heat rising from a hot pavement. In the blink of an eye, it disappeared right into thin air. I had a feeling it was going to be showing up in New York City any second.

And you know what? Before I moved here, none of this would have made any sense. Now nothing could surprise me.

Chapter Forty-One

Florida decided to sell off most of her shopping show stuff anyway, just to prove to herself and Grandpa Jack that she was a changed woman.

We spent the next few days sorting through her things, trying to decide what she wanted to sell and what she would keep. By the time Grandpa Jack pulled up on Flea Market Saturday, she told him to load up anything that was still in boxes, plus a whole lot more. Grandpa Jack was amazed.

"Are you sure 'bout all this, Florida?"

"Of course I'm sure, Jack. My TV shopping days are over," she said. "But I am not, under any circumstances, parting with my beauty products. That is where a woman must draw the line."

"Fine by me," said Grandpa Jack. And he swept her up in a great big kiss.

Grandpa had rented an enormous U-Haul moving truck, and we needed every square inch of it. We packed it until there wasn't a bit of room left and drove one last time to Big Daddy's Flea Market.

Buyers swarmed like bees. We didn't exactly bring in a million dollars, but it was enough money to make Florida happy. And you know what? I think she was actually glad to get rid of all those things.

"Sunshine, since this may be our last trip to Big Daddy's, howsabout you nose around and pick out something special for yourself?"

There were not a lot of things I wanted, and not a lot I needed. But what I did want couldn't be bought at any Flea Market.

I wanted Leroy.

When I told Grandpa Jack, he grinned. "Let's see what we can do."

It was early evening when we made it back to Truth or Consequences. We swung by the computer repair shop. Manny was just locking up for the night.

Grandpa tapped him on the shoulder and pulled out a wad of cash. He peeled off a $100 bill.

"We'd like to buy your dog," Grandpa said.

Manny stared at the money, dumbstruck. "Let me get this straight. You're *paying* me for that mangy mutt?"

"Yes, sir," said Grandpa. "Is that too much? We can offer you less."

"No, a hundred bucks is fine. He's all yours."

And he snapped the $100 bill right out of Grandpa's hand.

"Why anybody'd want him is a mystery to me," he muttered.

But he didn't know the real Leroy the way I did.

That night Florida cut up four juicy slices of meatloaf. She served three to us on her china plates at the dining room table, and put one piece in a bowl for Leroy. It was his very first dinner in his brand-new home.

"Mmm. Looks like your meatloaf is a big hit with Leroy too," said Grandpa Jack as he watched my new dog inhale his food.

"I have to tell you something, Jack. I didn't make it. All this time I've been buying the meatloaf from the deli counter at the Shur-Sav," Florida confessed.

"I've known that for years." Grandpa Jack shrugged. "It's still delicious, and you're still my best gal." Then he kissed her on the cheek.

And just for the record? This was the first time I'd been with my grandparents when there wasn't a single cross word between them.

August came quickly. The day before I was scheduled to leave for my vacation in Costa Rica, I gave Leroy a bath. Florida was going to take care of him while I was gone, and I wanted to make sure he wasn't stinky. When he was fluffy and dry, she suggested the three of us take a stroll around Truth or Consequences.

We walked along Grape Street into town. As we turned onto Date Street, Florida stopped in front of the Family Dollar Store.

"I'd like to buy you something," she said.

"No more buying, Florida."

"It's just one little thing. Besides, I am on a mission. You should know by now that when I'm on a mission there is simply no stopping me."

"I don't need any clothes." I was worried that maybe she'd try one last time to buy me something frilly and pink.

"No clothes. I know better than that."

She pushed open the glass door of the Dollar Store and marched inside. I followed, tugging Leroy on his leash. We headed straight to the back of the shop. Florida picked up a brand new regulation-sized soccer ball.

"I think this ball has your name on it, sweetie. Maybe when school starts you can join the soccer team."

I threw my arms around Florida, and she didn't care at all that I was wrinkling her shirt.

Back home I packed my suitcase. Then I lay on my bed, burying my face in my mom's old ferry jacket. If I really concentrated, its familiar scent of cinnamon and butterscotch had returned almost as strong as it was when she used to wear it on Bainbridge Island.

Florida triple-honked the horn of her gold Cadillac. I strapped on my backpack, grabbed my suitcase and ran outside. To me, the clouds overhead looked like dozens of Firebirds taking flight. And sailing among them was one billowy white guardian angel.

Leroy was going along for the ride, and he was curled up on the back seat. When I opened the car door he looked up at me, smiled wide, and thumped his tail. I think he was excited about my adventure.

My grandmother backed out of the driveway and we took off for the long drive to the El Paso Airport.

We headed south out of Truth or Consequences and onto the highway. I couldn't wait to see Rosalie Claire and to meet her new husband, Thomas. And here's the funny thing. I realized that I was actually going to miss my grandmother while I was gone. After all we'd been through, we had come to see each other in a whole new way.

So, with the help of a little magic, my life was turning out okay, after all.

We hadn't been driving long when my grandmother switched on the radio. "Dancing Queen" was playing. She sang along at the top of her lungs, and this time I sang along too.

Acknowledgments

There are so many people to thank. My husband Steve, who is my Number One sounding board and real-life alchemist.

David Skinner of ShadowCatcher Entertainment, for his unwavering belief in me and his love of Madison's indomitable spirit, that truly mirrors his own.

My agents, Mary Alice Kier and Anna Cottle of CineLit, who guided me down unfamiliar paths, and who were just as determined as I was to move Madison from the confines of my computer out into the larger world.

K.L. Going, for her keen and extensive editor's notes that helped me to carve away all the extra bits and craft a tighter story.

And for my first readers and good friends who returned with careful comments and enthusiastic support – Elana Lesser, Glenn Morrissey, Ann Reis, Nancy Stone, Char de Vasquez, and Elizabeth Mitchell. Their encouragement means the world to me.

I could thank each and every one of them a zillion times, and it still wouldn't be enough.